"I can't believe it," Claire said softly.

"The doctors always told us that if we put babies out of our minds, one might turn up unexpectedly, but I bet they never guessed it would happen this way."

"This wasn't how I pictured it, either," Adam replied.

After a few more minutes of gazing at the baby, she said, "Come and say hello to our little boy. He's so cute!"

"Don't get carried away, sweetheart. There's no way we can just assume the baby is ours...."

Will they...?

Won't they...?

Can they...?

The possibility of parenthood: for some couples
it's a seemingly impossible dream.
For others, it's an unexpected surprise....
Or perhaps it's a planned pregnancy
that brings a husband and wife closer together...
or turns their marriage upside down?

One thing is for sure, life will never be the same
when they find themselves having a baby...maybe!

This emotionally compelling miniseries
from Harlequin Romance® will warm your heart
and bring a tear to your eye....

THEIR
DOORSTEP BABY

Barbara Hannay

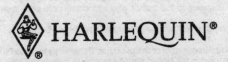

TORONTO • NEW YORK • LONDON
AMSTERDAM • PARIS • SYDNEY • HAMBURG
STOCKHOLM • ATHENS • TOKYO • MILAN • MADRID
PRAGUE • WARSAW • BUDAPEST • AUCKLAND

For Colleen

ISBN 0-373-03718-X

THEIR DOORSTEP BABY

First North American Publication 2002.

CHAPTER ONE

Early December—Sydney

ADAM TOWNSEND knew something was wrong. Very wrong. The moment he heard Claire's hasty footsteps enter the room he sensed it. Then he looked up and saw her deathly white face.

Even her lips were bleached of colour and her dark eyes shimmered with tears as she stared at him. She was clutching the timber door frame for support. What had happened? She looked ill—as fragile as a porcelain doll.

'Claire, what's the matter?' He scrambled to his feet, ignoring the cries of protest from his little nephews as he abandoned their noisy game of wrestling. 'What on earth's happened?'

'I think I've made a terrible mistake,' she whispered and her words brought fear clenching in his stomach like a cold and clammy fist.

Was this the moment he'd been dreading for weeks now? Had his wife's growing unhappiness finally pushed her to say something she'd regret? To do something they'd both regret?

'What kind of mistake?' he forced himself to ask.

But she seemed unable to answer. Her face crumpled as she shook her head and then she turned and left as quickly as she'd appeared.

'Stay here, guys,' he ordered the three little boys.

His heart rocketed into overdrive as he followed

Claire's stumbling progress back through her brother Jim's shabby cottage to the kitchen.

Jim and his wife Maria were both there, looking just as shocked and upset as Claire. Maria leant against her husband, one hand pressed to her mouth while the other held a slim rectangle of paper.

Adam recognised it instantly as a bank cheque and he had a sickening premonition that he could guess exactly what this was all about.

Maria's lips quivered. 'The baby,' she said, in a voice barely above a whisper. 'Claire has given us a cheque for Rosa.'

With an angry grunt, Jim shoved the cheque under Adam's nose and his heart leapt when he saw an alarming string of zeros. He whirled around to face Claire. 'You want to give all this to the baby?'

'Yes,' Claire said softly, but she didn't look at Adam and he knew why. She hadn't consulted him about this decision. Normally, they discussed everything—certainly anything as important as handing over such a large sum of money to Jim and Maria Tremaine's tiny, new daughter; the fifth baby the couple had produced in as many years.

'I wanted to help,' she told him and her voice seemed to crack beneath the weight of overpowering emotion.

'Come off the grass, sis,' Jim cried. 'You didn't just want to help. Tell Adam the whole story.'

Claire's lips trembled and tears spilled down her cheeks. 'It's—it's a kind of exchange.'

Oh, God! Adam's stomach dropped like a plane falling out of the sky. *Sweetheart, you can't be doing this!*

'An exchange for Rosa,' Maria clarified and then burst into tears.

'It's crazy!' Jim yelled. 'She wants to *buy* our baby!'

'I just wanted to help—to help you out.' Claire's tormented eyes sought Adam's. 'I'm sorry,' she whispered.

Bewildered, he shook his head. This disaster had happened in the ten short minutes he'd spent playing with his nephews. It was almost too much to take in. He'd never felt so torn. Part of him wanted to throw his arms around Claire and offer her comfort, but he also wanted to shake her.

Heaven knew, she was at the end of her tether, but this... She should never have done this.

'How could you want to take our little daughter away from us?' Jim glared.

Beside him, Maria continued to cry quietly.

Claire looked even more distressed. 'I thought—you have to struggle so hard to support so many children—and I—*we*—could give Rosa such a good home.'

Jim scowled. 'You two think we're in dire straits just because we don't eat caviar and smoked salmon and can't go gadding off to Europe whenever we flaming well feel like it?'

His jaw clenched stubbornly and he stepped closer to Maria and flung an arm across her shoulders. Drawing her against him, he planted a possessive kiss on her forehead.

Now Adam felt wretched that he hadn't shown Claire the same kind of solidarity. If anyone needed comforting, it was *his* wife. Despite his shock, he understood the wild, pitiful desperation that had driven her to this.

But if only she had spoken to me first.

She stood in the kitchen doorway looking miserable, guilty and lost with her arms wrapped across her stomach. And she continued to avoid his gaze.

But then her chin rose and she looked back at her brother with the same stubborn glare he'd fixed on her.

'I'd give up any luxury, any trip to Europe for a baby. You know how badly I want a baby of my own.'

Jim let out his breath noisily. 'Yeah, sis. I know it's rough on you.' He waved the cheque at her. 'But this—' Sadly, he shook his head. 'This is completely crazy. Apart from anything else, it's illegal.'

Then he held the cheque in both hands and slowly, deliberately ripped it into two pieces and then into four. He crossed the kitchen to the waste paper basket and let the pieces of paper flutter from his hand.

A choked cry broke from Claire's stricken lips. She turned to Adam. 'I didn't mean to hurt anyone,' she sobbed as she staggered across the room towards him. 'I'm sorry. I'm so sorry. What an awful, *awful* mess I've made.'

As she fell into his arms, one thought filled Adam's head: *I share the blame for this. The writing has been on the wall and I should have seen it coming.*

Five weeks earlier—thirty-seven thousand feet above the Indian Ocean

Claire wanted to kiss him now. Right now.

It wasn't the best moment to get such an urge. She was surrounded by other first class passengers and there were still many tedious hours left in the long flight from Sydney to Rome. Too much time to be plagued by wicked fantasies about the gorgeous man sitting right next to her.

She sighed as she studied his handsome, suntanned face. He was asleep and his head had fallen sideways so that his lips were temptingly close to hers.

Fixing her eyes on his sensuous mouth, she inched even closer and felt heat swell in her like a gathering storm. How badly she wanted to wake this man with a gentle kiss.

No, make that a hot and hungry kiss.

While she stared at him, her mind toyed with playful thoughts. She imagined the manly roughness of his overnight beard against her cheek, the silky feel of the dark hair that flopped across his brow, the delicious thrill of tracing her lips over the intriguing cleft in his chin.

Maybe if she concentrated hard enough, this wonderful creature would pick up on her thought waves. He might sense her intense interest and respond by taking her in his arms.

To heck with the other passengers.

As if on cue, his eyes opened and he smiled at her slowly. She couldn't resist leaning closer and immersing herself in the surprisingly deep, deep blue of his gaze.

'Hi there,' he said softly and he didn't move away.

'Hello.'

His eyes, edged by friendly laughter lines, were even more attractive than his mouth. Claire shivered with pleasure as they stared at each other.

With a little luck, her handsome neighbour would be blessed with an intuitive perception to match his good looks and he would kiss her within the next thirty seconds.

Her face grew hot with anticipation. Her breathing picked up pace.

If he doesn't kiss me now…

The gods were smiling. He reached towards her and his hands gently cradled her cheeks.

Thank heavens…

The laughter lines around his eyes deepened as he smiled at her while his approving gaze assessed her hair and face, finally focusing on her mouth. 'Do you always look this good in the—' quickly he glanced at his wrist-watch '—in the afternoon?'

'Of course,' she replied in a breathy little voice, 'but I look even better in the morning.'

'How promising.'

He kissed her. And, boy, could he kiss! His lips were tender…and teasing. His mouth was tantalising… and…his kiss was slow…she was drowning…just a little dizzy…she'd been wanting this so much.

'Mr and Mrs Townsend?'

Claire and Adam sprang apart. A flight attendant, carrying a tray of glasses filled with champagne, stood in the aisle beside them. Her expression was polite, although her eyes danced with curiosity. 'Would you care for a little celebration? We're about to cross the Equator.'

'Champagne?' Claire asked shakily. 'Why not?' She struggled to sit sedately and her hands flew to her cloud of blonde hair.

Adam reached past her and accepted their glasses of pale, fizzing wine. The attendant hovered for a moment, eyeing him with frank interest before moving on.

Clinking his glass against Claire's, Adam murmured, 'Here's to my audacious and irresistible wife. Happy holiday.'

'Happy holiday,' Claire replied softly.

He leaned closer and whispered in her ear, 'You were pretending we'd just met, weren't you?'

'You pretended you didn't know how I look in the afternoon. You were happy to play your part,' she reminded him.

'Of course I was. More than happy.' He grinned. 'Let's hope this holiday gives us a chance to play out all your fantasies.'

Then he kissed her again.

She smiled and, sinking back into the upholstered seat, sipped her champagne. How lucky she was. Eight years of marriage to a gorgeous, sexy man. How lucky they both were that their marriage was so special, an equal partnership and yet so much fun.

Passionate lovers, best of friends, happy travelling companions, sharing joint interests in Nardoo, their outback cattle property...on every level their relationship was perfect.

On *almost* every level.

The negative thought came, as it always did, like an unexpected and vicious attack from behind. Claire set her glass on the tray in front of her and her hand was already shaking.

Closing her eyes, she tried to block out the sudden, sickening sadness that threatened. Not now. She didn't want to think about *that* now. She and Adam were embarking on a special, wonderful holiday.

They both loved Italy. And this time, when Adam finished his meetings with European beef importers, they were planning to linger in Florence...Venice...Rome... absorbing the magnificent art, the splendid cathedrals, the restaurants and the music. It was going to be superb and she wanted to stay buoyed up and happy.

Silently she repeated the mantra that had been echoing in her head for days now. *It's going to happen this time. I'm going to fall pregnant. By the time we get home, I'll be pregnant.* And once again she promised herself that she wouldn't allow a single negative thought to spoil the holiday.

Surely the relaxing weeks ahead would work their magic...

Surely this month...this time...

'Are you OK?' Adam asked.

She nodded, not trusting herself to look his way when she knew that, despite her hopeful thoughts, her eyes were already filming with the threat of annoying tears. *Think about something else, woman! Anything else! Don't spoil things now!*

Reaching into the pocket in the seat in front of her, she pulled out the murder mystery she'd bought at the airport bookshop in Sydney. The story was rather good and it was just getting to the thrilling climax. With a little luck it would divert her mind away from that dreaded subject.

She'd used her boarding pass as a bookmark and now she opened at chapter ten and, taking another deep sip of champagne, began to read.

Adam stood on the elegant balcony of their hotel suite and stared thoughtfully at the dignified old city stretched before him. Rome at night was like a prima donna commanding centre stage.

There couldn't be a place on earth more different from the wide, open plains and grey-blue-green bush of his home in western Queensland. Here there was so much man-made grandeur. So much power had been won and lost within this city's ancient walls.

He stretched his arms above his head and rolled his big shoulders, trying to ease the lingering tension in his muscles after the long trip.

His athletic build was testimony to the hard life he lived in the Australian outback. He was used to the physical demands of running thousands of head of cattle on ten thousand square kilometres of wilderness. Sitting for hours cooped up on a plane left him feeling restless.

From behind him came the sounds of splashing. Claire was in the luxurious *en suite* bathroom, relishing a long, soothing soak in scented bath oils.

He smiled and thought about joining her. But as he stepped back through the French doors into their bedroom, slap bang on top of that pleasant thought came an unwelcome surge of anxiety. Was Claire pinning too much hope on this holiday? He had a horrible suspicion that her whole focus on this trip away would be to produce a baby.

If it didn't happen…?

He drew a huge breath, holding it for long seconds and letting it go noisily. The doctor had warned them not to expect too much. There was every chance this holiday wouldn't produce the result Claire longed for and he was finding it harder and harder to console her when the baby blues struck.

He groaned. Damn it, he should be able to comfort his wife.

He loved Claire.

How could he not love her? She was lovely to look at and even lovelier to hold.

And the things he'd learned about her since their marriage had proved that she was his perfect life partner. Her delight in passionate lovemaking was an ongoing miracle, but, even more miraculously, she shared his intense interest in their property, Nardoo.

Most importantly, she was his best mate. *She was fun!*

After eight years, he knew and cherished every quirky detail of her personality and he'd always felt their relationship was rock solid in spite of their intense disappointment at not being able to have a baby of their own.

But just lately he'd felt a niggle of fear that perhaps Claire didn't love him quite as completely as he loved her. He tried to tell himself he was wrong. How could he doubt her feelings after all these years?

He knew she loved him. She showed it in so many ways.

But her need for a baby was becoming desperate.

Heaven knew, he'd wanted a baby, too. In the bleak months that had followed his parents' death in a light plane crash, the possibility that he and Claire would produce future generations of Townsends to inherit Nardoo had provided a measure of consolation.

But when the likelihood of babies had grown increasingly slim, he'd come to terms with that disappointment. He refused to give up hope, but he also knew that as long as he had Claire, he could still be happy.

She didn't seem to feel that way. Lately, her longing was bordering on obsession, as if the idea of having a baby was the single most important thing in her life.

And more frequently these days, it left Adam feeling on the outside.

There was a click behind him and the bathroom door slid open. Claire, wrapped in a huge cherry-red bath towel, came slowly towards him across the thick cream carpet.

Her loose curls were caught on top of her head by a chunky plastic clip. Her face, cleaned of all make-up, looked fresh and astonishingly beautiful.

With gentle fingers, she reached up and touched his cheek. 'You look a bit down in the mouth. Are you OK?'

'Sure,' he said, turning to kiss the inner curve of her hand. 'Just tired.'

'Long flights are the pits, aren't they?' She kept her hand there, cupping his face as she traced her thumb slowly along his jaw and he saw her mouth quirk into a secretive, sexy little smile.

'It's too bad you're tired,' she said softly as she trailed

her hand down from his jaw to the inside of his open-necked shirt.

Her deep brown eyes were lit by a purposeful light. They glimmered, seductive and teasing. The message was unmistakable and Adam's thoughts scrambled instantly.

Desire pulsed and surged through him. 'Did I mention the word tired?' he asked with a slow grin. 'Of course, I'm not tired at all, but I'll take a shower.'

'You can shower later.'

Laughing, loving her, Adam reached forward, but with a playful laugh of her own she suddenly slipped daintily out of his reach and raised a hand to halt him.

'Whoa, there!' she teased, smiling.

She raised her other hand, undid the clasp that secured the knot of curls and slowly shook her soft blonde hair free. Then, just as slowly, she tossed the clip in the air. It bounced behind her onto the carpet as she propped both her hands on her hips and arched her back so that her breasts thrust cheekily forward.

Adam's insides took a tumble-turn as the loose knot holding her towel slipped undone and it slid past her hips to the floor.

'Ah—that feels better,' she murmured.

His grin collapsed. With a breathless growl he closed the gap between them, and this time Claire offered no resistance when he hauled her close.

Hungrily, his hands found the lush curves of her naked bottom and he pulled her hard against the clamouring need of his arousal. '*This* feels a whole lot better,' he assured her.

Claire's fingers worked nimbly to undo the buttons of his shirt. 'We'll feel even better when you get rid of these.'

Oh, yes! 'My wife is a shameless hussy,' he murmured

against her neck. She smelled so good—of something exotic—maybe sandalwood and flowers.

'You're not complaining, are you?'

'Not a word of complaint, sweetheart.' *Not one single word!*

His body throbbed with an almost painful urgency as he walked her backwards towards the enormous bed. When they reached it, their gazes meshed and Claire gave a little cry of excited surprise as he pushed her gently, so that she fell to the mattress with a light bounce.

With the briefest shrug of his shoulders, the shirt she'd unbuttoned dropped to the floor and he smiled down at her as she lay on the bed, her skin still glowing from the bath. After eight years, he would never grow tired of looking at this woman.

Flaring heat mounted even more insistently in his loins as he undid his belt buckle.

And watched her.

Watched her watching him…while he unsnapped the fastener on his jeans. Her eyes smouldered with a familiar, heated promise as his jeans and boxer shorts slid to the floor.

But then he paused.

For a tantalising, breathless minute, he delayed touching her while he deliberately took his time, delighting in a slow visual appreciation of her loveliness.

Her hair shimmered like a softly glowing candle against the midnight-blue silk of the bedspread. Her chocolate-brown eyes were dark with longing, her soft mouth was slightly parted to reveal a glimpse of white teeth. An impatient pulse beat in the delicate hollow at the base of her pale throat.

'Do I still look OK in the evenings?' she asked, huskily. His breath caught with a sharp in-drawn hiss as his gaze rested on the pretty, feminine lushness of her pink-tipped breasts and the smooth, pale skin of her slim waist, then, finally, her softly rounded hips and thighs, her long, slender legs.

'You know you're quite something,' he said, his voice sounding as low and choked as hers. 'In the mornings you look *very* OK. In the afternoons you look exception-ally OK, but in the evenings you look *so* OK I can't think straight.'

'So...' Her eyes flashed a cheeky challenge. 'Stop thinking.'

Her gaze slid down his body, returning his appraising look with one of her own. 'You look much more than OK,' she announced with a proprietorial grin. 'You look sensational.' Her arms reached out to him. 'And, my dear man, you're *all* mine.'

Supporting his weight with his hands on either side of her, he lowered his head to kiss her. They reached to-wards each other and their mouths met. Their lips and tongues merged and the kiss felt hauntingly familiar—lingering and loving—like a mixture of all their yester-days.

'You're so right, my girl,' he whispered. 'I'm all yours. Only yours.'

'That's so good to know.'

He kissed her again and this kiss quickly turned fe-verish—deep and blazing—as full of alluring promise as tomorrow.

And at last, as his hands, trembling with desire, laid claim to her feminine bounty, he caressed her, loving her with the bold assurance of a man who understood com-pletely all the intimate ways his woman longed to be touched.

From beneath half-shut lids, he saw Claire's cheeks

grow more flushed and he heard the soft moan of her excitement. He felt her hips lift and arch and his stomach took off in a high, curving dive.

'Oh, Adam,' she whispered. 'Love me. I need you so badly.'

And faced with that sweet command, Adam let any shadowy doubts roll away.

CHAPTER TWO

'I'VE lit a candle to St Anthony.' Claire's face shone as she joined Adam at the little sidewalk café.

They had spent three weeks in Europe now, first attending a series of conferences and seminars in various centres and then exploring northern Italy. Now they were spending half a day in Padua before catching a train across to Florence.

Adam had been wandering through the grounds of Padua's famous university while Claire visited yet another church.

'Any particular reason you chose St Anthony?' he queried as a waiter served them coffee and pizza.

'I found a brochure that says many infertile couples pin their hopes on him. They come to his church here in Padua especially.' She reached forward and gripped Adam by the arm. 'It claims that St Anthony has performed many amazing miracles. Maybe you should have come with me.'

Adam suppressed an urge to comment and took a deep draft of scalding coffee instead. He feared their holiday wasn't working out quite as well as he'd hoped. Sure, Claire was enjoying the sights, she was bright and lively company.

But she's not letting go!

On this trip she was meant to be following their doctor's advice—relaxing completely—forgetting about the urgent need to prove her fertility.

The doctor had been quite firm. 'You'll stand a better

chance if you can take things more calmly,' he'd told them. 'Some people can try too hard for a baby. Sometimes an intense yearning for a positive result can have the opposite effect.'

But Claire seemed to be more focused on her infertility than ever. If she wasn't lighting candles in churches, she was buying expensive gifts for her sister-in-law Maria, or her children.

She'd spent hours selecting toys or clothes she would have loved to buy for her own child, if she'd had one.

As far as he could tell, she hadn't bought anything for herself. In Venice, she'd found an exquisite glass angel and he'd thought she was going to indulge herself.

'Isn't this the most beautiful thing you've ever seen?' she cried and her eyes glowed with joy.

Picturing it on the mantelpiece in Nardoo's homestead, he agreed.

But as Claire carried it back to their hotel, she said, 'I'm going to give this angel to Maria. I know she'd love it. And when we stop in Siena, I want to buy her a *panettone*. I'm sure she'd love an authentic Italian Christmas cake.'

What bothered him most about Claire's preoccupation with Maria and her children was that he knew what lay behind it. Any day now, their sister-in-law was due to give birth to her fifth baby. Five kids!

It seemed she and Jim hadn't yet figured out how those little ankle-biters started.

Claire tried to pretend that she wasn't jealous of Maria—that she was happy for the younger woman. But Adam was quite sure that, beneath the cheery façade, she was growing more depressed and miserable.

And there was too damn little he could do about it.

*　　*　　*

The train journey to Florence took them through the beautiful hills of Tuscany. As the countryside rushed past them in a late autumn blur of red and gold flashes, Claire relaxed with her head on Adam's broad shoulder and admired the spectacle through the train's window.

But her heart set up a fretful pumping when the mobile phone in his coat pocket suddenly beeped. She swung upright, and her fingers dug into her palms as she watched him retrieve the phone. She studied his face carefully while he listened to his caller.

It could be simply a business call, but she fancied she could hear Jim's voice. Her brother always felt he had to shout when he dialled long distance.

After a long period of listening, Adam said, 'That's great. Congratulations, mate. Thanks for letting us know and give our love to Maria.'

Her face flamed as he depressed the button and looked at her with eyes awash with gentle concern. 'Maria's had a little girl.'

'How lovely,' she whispered. 'What are they going to call her?'

'Rosa.'

To her dismay, she burst into tears. 'Rosa is such a s-sweet name,' she sobbed. 'Another little g-girl. Oh, Adam, they have five babies. I don't think I can bear it.'

Desperately, she tried to stem the flow of tears, but it seemed impossible. How embarrassing! Passengers were staring at her. But she couldn't stop crying and the view of the beautiful Tuscan countryside was completely obscured.

Adam held her tenderly and she was so grateful for that, especially as she knew he couldn't really understand how she felt. No one seemed to understand what it was like to be jealous of people who had babies and then to feel guilty about that jealousy.

Adam could never really understand her awful sense of emptiness, as if she had a great gaping void inside her. He didn't know the way her arms ached to hold a little warm baby.

He'd always been incredibly matter-of-fact and fatalistic about their situation. He'd gone through all the horrible, invasive tests with her, but when they'd been told there was nothing medically wrong with either of them—that there was nothing operable or treatable the doctors could correct—Adam had accepted the news.

For him it was easy to accept that if a pregnancy was meant to happen it would, if not, so be it. But for Claire it was much harder. She was so attuned to her cycles. Her physical and emotional awareness of her own body was so intense that each month, when she knew she'd failed yet again, she felt frozen inside.

She hated that feeling of emptiness. Of failure. She dreaded it. And she was so scared it was going to happen again.

After an age, she was able to lift her damp face from Adam's shoulder, to wipe her tears and paste a brave smile on her face. But then she was swamped by a fresh wave of remorse. Poor Adam! She was wrecking his holiday with such hysterical carryings on.

By the time they reached Florence, she was determined not to mention Maria's baby—or anyone's baby, for that matter. Over the next few days, she riveted her attention on Adam and on the wonderfully rich feast of art in the cathedrals, the piazzas and the galleries.

She and Adam shared happy kisses on the Ponte Vecchio, the romantic bridge crossing the River Arno that had inspired poets for centuries. They held hands as they strolled and lingered through the straw markets.

In the evenings they ate out, sharing exquisite meals like gnocchi gorgonzola that melted in their mouths, and they drank rich red Italian wine. Back at their hotel, they made love long into the night.

On the morning they were to leave for Assisi, she went to the bathroom and saw the stain she'd been dreading.

No! Oh, Lord, no! It couldn't be.

Sitting on the edge of the bathtub, she let the tears fall. She tried desperately to cry quietly. She didn't want Adam to hear her. But she couldn't bear the disappointment.

Her prayers hadn't been answered. Their relaxing holiday hadn't helped. Once again, her world had stopped.

Another chance lost.

Eight years of marriage without a baby.

It was some time before she felt strong enough to come out of the bathroom. Adam looked at her sharply. 'Everything OK?' he asked.

She couldn't speak at first, but she nodded.

'Are you sure, Claire? You don't look well.'

'I'm fine. Really I am.' She was not going to make a fuss about this. Adam didn't deserve to be subjected to her fits of depression. Fighting back a fresh threat of tears, she hurried towards the doorway, mumbling that there was one last thing she wanted to buy.

He caught her hand as she passed. 'Would you like me to come with you?'

'No,' she answered hastily, shaking her hand free again. 'You finish your packing. I'm just going to Via Ghibellina. There's something I saw in a little shop there. I won't be long.'

With a gentle touch, he brushed his finger down her cheek and his eyes held hers.

He knows. Claire looked away, afraid to let him see how upset she felt.

'You know, you're the prettiest girl in this whole damn town,' he said with an encouraging smile.

'Sure,' she replied and managed a hasty answering grimace that she hoped would pass for a smile.

Hurrying out of the hotel and through the streets, she took deep breaths and forced herself to calm down. The tiny pink layette hand-stitched by nuns was still there in the shop window. Yesterday, she'd almost bought it to put away with the things she was keeping for her baby. If only she'd bought it then!

Now it was too late. No matter how much she wanted to, she couldn't bring herself to keep it. Today she was buying it for Rosa.

The old woman in the shop wrapped the dainty garments very carefully in blue and white tissue paper. Claire carried the parcel back to the hotel and didn't show it to Adam. But she was aware of him watching her, silent and frowning, as she slipped it into her suitcase along with the presents she'd selected for the rest of Jim's family.

'I'm packed and ready,' she said when she finished, but for the life of her she couldn't manage another smile.

'Auntie Claire! Uncle Adam!'

'Mum, they're here!'

Claire could hear the excited cries of her nephews even before she and Adam made their way across the porch, past the row of dead pot plants, to the front door of Jim and Maria's house in suburban Sydney.

This stopover in Sydney before travelling another two

thousand kilometres to Nardoo had been her idea. She knew Adam was having second thoughts about the wisdom of visiting Jim's family. He was worried that seeing the new baby would get her worked up. But she was determined to be strong.

The last few days in Italy had been wonderful and she'd worked hard to get over her disappointment. Now that they were home again, she would get on with her life. She would calmly congratulate Jim and Maria on the newest addition to their family and hand over the gifts. And that would be all. No fuss. No tears.

Before she could knock against the peeling paint, the door opened and a trio of eager little faces beamed up at them.

'Hello, darlings!' Claire bent low, opened her arms to Tony, Luke and Toto and was swamped with boisterous hugs and kisses. 'My, look at you. You're all growing far too quickly.'

Over their heads she saw her sister-in-law, Maria, coming towards her with her sweet toddler Francesca in her arms. Claire kissed Maria and thought she looked pale and tired. How could she not be tired with this house full of demanding little people?

And now there was another.

She entered the house and looked around her, her stomach bunching nervously. She could do this! There was no sign of a bassinet and she wasn't sure if she was relieved or disappointed.

When Tony had been born, the bassinet had stayed proudly in this front room so that every visitor had to tiptoe and whisper while they admired Jim and Maria Tremaine's son and heir.

She guessed that the new baby must be tucked away

from her noisy brothers and sister, asleep in a back bedroom.

Behind her, Adam piled the gifts they'd brought onto a coffee-table, while Tony and Luke tried to tackle him to the floor for their favourite uncle sport—wrestling. He'd always been a great hit with his nephews.

'Hold on, tigers, let me say hello to your mother first,' he said, laughing.

As he ducked his dark head to kiss Maria's cheek, Claire noticed that even her careworn sister-in-law brightened with a spark of feminine interest.

Adam always had an instantaneous effect on women— any woman, any age—and every time Claire saw it, she marvelled that she'd been the lucky one he'd wanted to marry.

'Jim's probably still fighting his way through the peak-hour traffic, but, please, sit down,' Maria said.

Claire wanted to ask about the new baby, but instead she took her seat and pointed to the gifts. 'We brought you some souvenirs that can't wait till Christmas and there's a *panettone* from Siena.'

An image of the narrow, ancient, cobbled streets of Siena, dark and crowded in by tall medieval buildings, flashed through her mind as she handed Maria the boxed traditional cake and she felt a pang of sympathy for her brother's wife, who had never seen the fascinating homeland of her family.

'Thank you,' Maria said, waiting until her guests were seated before she took her place in an old lounge chair. 'Did you like Italy?' She frowned as she tried to poke some stuffing back through a tear in the upholstery.

'We loved it,' Claire said gently. 'We've brought you lots of photos.'

The children, their dark eyes big with excitement,

crowded closer and it seemed as good a time as any to hand out all the things she and Adam had brought for the family. For the next few moments there was a flurry of unwrapping and cries of delight.

Maria set Claire's gift, the delicate Venetian glass angel, on the sideboard and Claire felt a stab of discomfort as she noticed that it looked sadly out of place next to the roughly painted nativity scene the children had made from play dough. In this little house, it suddenly looked as unsuitable and showy as an exotic orchid in a bunch of humble field daisies.

The little layette she'd bought in Florence was left till last.

'This is for the baby,' Claire said, handing Maria the slim parcel wrapped in tissue paper and hoping no one noticed how her hands shook.

'Oh,' gasped Maria as she pulled the tissue aside and drew out the contents. She held the dainty garments out in front of her. 'How—how exquisite.'

Tony ran to his mother's side. 'Rosa will look like a baby princess.'

Claire and Adam exchanged a quick glance and Claire read mild concern in her husband's eyes. She looked again at the delicate baby clothes trimmed with exquisite hand-stitched embroidery and then at her sister-in-law's simple cotton dress that had gone out of fashion at least five summers ago.

Her eyes strayed to the hovering circle of happy, bright-eyed children. Their feet were bare and they all wore obvious hand-me-downs—tee shirts and shorts, faded from much washing.

Claire compressed her lips tightly as she realised how impractical she'd been. Maria wouldn't have time to hand wash and take special care of this delicate baby wear.

Rosa would no doubt spend her first long, sizzling summer in their hot little box of a house, dressed in little more than a nappy and a cotton singlet.

'I couldn't resist it,' she said weakly.

'It's beautiful. Thank you so much. Rosa will wear it to mass on Christmas Day and be the best-dressed baby in Sydney.'

Maria's eyes shone warmly and Claire felt a little better. She looked again to Adam for support, but he'd finally succumbed to a wrestling match on the floor with Tony and Luke. The two boys were gleefully bouncing on top of him while little Toto watched and cheered.

Before she could indulge in second thoughts about the suitability of her gifts, a lot of things happened quickly. Jim strolled through the front door with a six-pack of beer under his arm. Toto tried to join the wrestling, banged his head on the corner of the coffee table and began to bellow loudly. The telephone rang and a tiny little wail sounded from down the hallway.

After a quick 'Hi, sis,' and a peck on the cheek, Jim dealt with the phone call. Only Maria could console Toto.

'Would you like me to see to the baby?' Claire asked.

Maria looked at her over the top of Toto's curly head. Her eyes were underlined by heavy, dark circles. She looked dreadfully tired. 'Thanks,' she mouthed above her little boy's wails.

And as Claire crossed the room before heading down the hall she fancied she saw tears in Maria's eyes.

The baby's cries were coming from the main bedroom at the back of the house. As soon as Claire entered the darkened room, her eyes flew to the bassinet in the corner by the curtained window.

Making her way around the bed, she stepped over a mattress on the floor. No doubt it was where Francesca slept. Then she held her breath as she saw the tiny form in the basket.

Rosa Claire Tremaine, just a few weeks old.

She couldn't help her reaction. Her throat grew painfully choked and her eyes brimmed with a rush of hot tears as she stepped closer.

The little baby lay on her side in the simple, unadorned crib. There wasn't even a ribbon threaded through the cane work and, as Claire had guessed she would be, the tiny girl was dressed in a simple white singlet and nappy.

Her little face was red and screwed up with the effort of crying. Claire stared at her, taking in every detail. Her head was covered by the sweetest cap of fuzzy brown hair—her dainty little limbs, hands and feet, were pink and perfect, as were her ears. Her little chest was rising and falling.

Rosa was a miniature miracle.

'Such a sad little girl,' Claire cried as she bent down and carefully lifted the sobbing baby. Her heart swelled with emotion as she held the warm, minuscule body against her. She supported Rosa's weight with one hand, while her other hand gently stroked her super-soft skin.

Almost immediately the cries subsided into little snuffles. Claire pressed her lips to the back of the tiny girl's neck and her nostrils were filled with the unique, intoxicating smell of new baby.

Like a snugly puppy or kitten, Rosa's head nestled against the curve of Claire's shoulder and, with her open mouth, the tiny baby nuzzled her neck.

Claire hardly knew how to cope with the flood of unexpected love she felt for this sweet little creature. Oh, God! She wanted to be brave, but her arms were so starved for the feel of a warm, live baby. There'd been an aching hole inside her for so long, and now her heart almost broke with the bittersweet pain of her longing.

Even though she and Adam hadn't bothered about a family during the first three years of their marriage, she'd endured five years of trying since then. *Sixty months* of disappointment and unbearably empty arms.

And here was Maria, so much younger, and for each of those five years she'd produced a baby. Maria only had to look at Jim and she was pregnant! Five of them! It wasn't fair.

It wasn't fair at all.

'If you were mine,' Claire whispered as she rocked Rosa gently, 'I'd make you such a sweet little nursery in our home at Nardoo. I'd have the cutest baby things for you—the prettiest clothes—lovely soft talcum powder and baby creams for your delicate baby skin. I'd look after you so beautifully.'

She glanced over her shoulder and caught sight of herself in the age-speckled mirror above the dressing table. Looking back at her was a tall, slim woman with big brown eyes and a delicate but sad face, surrounded by a mass of soft, light golden curls.

Surely I look like a normal, nice enough woman who deserves to be a mother?

Her eyes lingered over the most wonderful part of that picture, the dear little baby curled in her arms. Rosa looked so perfect, so *perfectly* at home as she snuggled against her breast.

A fierce pain speared Claire's chest. It felt as if someone had plucked at her very heartstrings.

'I'd set up a rocking-chair on the veranda and we'd sit there and watch Adam riding home at the end of a long, hard day in the outback,' she whispered. 'You'd love it up there in the bush. You could help me to feed all the pretty, noisy parrots that fly in at sundown.'

The baby's snuffles stopped. It was almost as if she were listening to Claire.

'There's a pied butcher bird that taps on the kitchen window every morning for his breakfast,' she told her. 'And when you're bigger, you can play in the beautiful garden I've made at Nardoo. Adam will buy you a dear little pony and we can both teach you to ride.'

She knew Adam would be a fantastic father. The best father in the world! It would be so wonderful.

Claire kissed the back of the baby's little head again and she couldn't stop the tears from spilling down her cheeks. No one understood her pain.

No one.

A throat-clearing sound from the doorway startled her. Adam was standing there, watching her, frowning. He stepped into the room and walked towards her, his mouth tilting into an uncertain smile.

He looked at the baby in her arms.

'She's so sweet, isn't she?' she whispered.

'Yeah,' he agreed. Gingerly, he reached out one finger and touched the tiny hand that lay curled on Claire's shoulder and then he touched Claire's tear-stained cheek. 'Were you imagining she's yours?'

As Adam asked the question he looked so troubled, Claire's tears erupted into proper, loud sobs.

'My sweet girl,' he whispered as his big arms came around her and the baby. 'Hey, there. Don't cry. You mustn't cry. You'll upset the baby.'

But in spite of her determination to be strong, she couldn't stop crying. She leant her head against Adam's chest and sobbed her heart out, sobbed for all those long, empty months she'd waited for a baby. Sobbed for her recent disappointment and all the unbearable months still to come.

And she felt her husband's strong arms holding her close and his lips pressed against her forehead, but, to her horror, she knew that this time his loving embrace couldn't bring her the comfort she needed.

There was only one person who could ease her terrible pain—and it was this little baby in her arms.

CHAPTER THREE

AS THEIR taxi sped through the dark streets, taking Adam and Claire through Sydney's suburbs and back to their hotel, they sat silently and stiffly apart on the back seat. Claire stole anxious glances Adam's way and once, when they were passing beneath a street light, their eyes met and she saw pain and stark worry in his.

An answering stab of anguish twisted in her chest. How could she ever live down her shame? She'd asked her brother if she could *buy* his baby!

How had she ever imagined that Maria and Jim would be relieved and pleased with her offer? What a fruit cake she was! Why hadn't she seen that they would find her offer shocking, even insulting?

She'd totally lost it!

The impulse to ask for Rosa hadn't been rationally thought out. It had seized her with frightening speed and, once it had taken hold, she'd reacted quickly, not giving herself time for second thoughts.

For a brief, shining moment it had seemed like a brilliant solution to everyone's problems.

Her brother and his wife were really struggling to support their family. Maria looked very tired and strained. Their house was bursting at the seams. And it wasn't as if they wouldn't be able to see Rosa whenever they wanted to.

But how quickly that shining idea had dimmed. Now it could go on record as the blackest plan ever hatched.

The taxi swung sharply around a corner and Claire

shoved a fist against her mouth to hold back a sob. She didn't want to cry again. She was so sick of crying.

What a mess she'd made of things! And she'd hurt Adam, too. She could tell by the grim set of his mouth that he was still very upset.

Leaning back against the seat, she closed her eyes, but tears insisted on seeping from beneath her lids as she remembered the look on his face when he'd realised what she'd done.

'You're not in this alone,' he'd reminded her and she'd felt a horrible pang of guilt.

Rushing headlong into making the offer without even consulting Adam was yet another example of how thoughtless she'd been this evening.

She had apologised later, after they'd made their uncomfortable farewells to Jim and Maria and were walking back down the uneven garden path to the waiting taxi, but she had the horrible feeling that her apology had been too little, too late.

For the first time in her marriage, she felt as if a tiny but irreparable rift had broken the tightly woven fabric of their bond.

Claire swiped at her damp eyes with the backs of her hands. She would feel better if she thought it were possible for Jim or Maria to understand what had made her behave that way. But there was no way they could imagine what it was like to be trying for a baby for years and years…and years.

Not even Adam really understood how she felt. He hadn't experienced the deadening, inner desolation she suffered when, month after tedious month, she was forced to accept that her womb was empty *again*…

She wanted him to understand. She needed him to, but she feared it was asking too much of her husband. This problem of infertility just wasn't the same for a man as it was for a woman.

No one labelled a man *barren*.

Just thinking about that brought a wave of self-pity sweeping over her and she was still feeling sorry for herself when their taxi glided up the impressive column-lined drive to their hotel's entrance.

Adam paid the driver, but, instead of slipping her arm companionably through his as she usually did, Claire marched stiffly in front of him through the automatic sliding glass doors and across the polished marble foyer.

In the lift they stood staring blankly ahead in brittle, uncomfortable silence.

As soon as the door of their room swung shut behind them, she turned to her husband, bracing herself for his attack. 'I know you're very angry,' she countered quickly. 'I'm sorry I made such a dreadful scene. I didn't stop to think how much my offer would hurt Jim and Maria. You must be so ashamed of me.'

Adam sighed as he dropped his wallet and a set of keys onto the little table at his side of the bed. 'I'm not ashamed of you, Claire.'

'But you're upset.'

'I'm disappointed that you rushed in and offered Maria and Jim that money without talking it over first.'

Emotion constricted Claire's throat. She should have known Adam would be decent about this when he had every right to be angry, to lecture her. Illogical as it was, the fact that he was exercising so much self-control made her feel worse.

She forced her eyes wide open to hold tears at bay. She was determined not to cry, but it was so hard. She wondered if she'd sprung a leak.

'I didn't have time to talk it over with you,' she tried

to explain, conscious that it was a rather weak excuse. 'The idea only hit me tonight and—and I couldn't help myself, Adam. I felt I had to act straight away.'

'But rushing in like that without talking to me. It's as if I just don't count. It's sure as hell not the way I want to become a father.'

'Oh, Adam.' Claire's voice broke on a sob. 'I'm so sorry.' She drew in a deep breath. 'But I'm afraid our— our problem—this whole infertility deal—is so much harder for me than you.'

Adam undid the top buttons on his shirt. 'What makes you so sure about that?'

In a gesture she realised was overly grand, Claire flung her hands out to her sides. 'It doesn't dominate a man's thinking the way it does a woman's and society doesn't have the same expectations for men to produce babies.'

The slight movement of his mouth might have been an attempt at a smile. 'I always understood that men played an admittedly small but vital part in the quest for babies. I *thought* you'd noticed.'

Claire groaned. Trust Adam to remind her how much she enjoyed his lovemaking. The most upsetting thing about this whole business was that their sex life could be so powerful and beautiful and yet…so fruitless.

'Of course you play a role.' Any other time she would have been able to turn this moment into a friendly joke. A joke that would lead to laughter and love.

Not tonight. Tonight she'd lost sight of her sense of humour. 'You have to admit that where pregnancy is concerned, ultimately, it's a woman's responsibility to come up with the goods.'

Adam walked towards her then. He came around the foot of the bed and reached for her and drew her towards him. 'Sweetheart,' he murmured sadly. 'We've been over this before. You know you mustn't blame yourself.'

With his arms around her, he caressed the side of her head with his jaw. In the past, Claire had always loved the way he did that. She loved the way they fitted together as if they'd been custom-built for each other. She loved the feel of him, especially in the evening when his chin was just a little raspy with the beginnings of stubble.

She wanted to enjoy it again. She wanted to relent and to melt against him, to absorb her husband's love. But tonight she was too tense and too full of self-recrimination to yield to his touch. Even though she hated herself for doing it, she remained standing stiffly in his arms.

'We've discussed this over and over,' he said.

'But, Adam,' she answered in a hollow, toneless voice that echoed exactly how she felt, 'if I can't have a baby, my whole life feels meaningless. What on earth is the use of being a woman if I can't fulfil the main reason I was put on this earth?'

He let her go then and stepped back a little and a kind of resigned bleakness crept back into his eyes. 'I think you're being melodramatic, Claire. We're still young and you shouldn't give up hope.'

'It's too hard to keep hoping.'

'Then look around you. There are many, many women who never have a baby and who live fulfilled, useful lives.'

'But I'm not one of them!'

'How can you—how can you be so certain?'

Claire sighed.

'Adam, in my head I know you're right. But my emotions tell me something else. Deep down I'm sure I'm *meant* to have a baby of my own.'

'Oh, Claire—'

The tears welled and spilled. 'I know I'm meant to be a mother, otherwise I wouldn't feel this awful, aching, ongoing emptiness. That's what made me do what I did tonight. I held Rosa and—and I—I lost it.'

'I know, Claire. I know.' Gently he kissed the top of her head and his fingers stroked the back of her neck.

But he couldn't offer her any solution apart from his love. It should have been enough. She knew that. But tonight…why, oh, why wasn't it enough tonight?

They prepared for bed and, when they slipped between the sheets, Adam didn't try to seduce her. He kissed her and held her, massaged her tense shoulders and murmured soothing talk, but eventually he drifted away into sleep.

And Claire lay in the dark, tossing and turning, swamped with guilt. She kept seeing Maria's stricken face and hearing her final words… 'If you ever have a baby, you will understand. It's too much to ask a mother to give her baby away. You're asking the impossible. I'd rather starve than lose one of my little ones.'

If you ever have a baby… Those words echoed over and over in her head and they left her with the same desolate hollowness she'd felt this evening when she'd held Rosa. But now there was the bitter aftertaste of shame as well.

'I've decided to start another garden. We need something more on the western side,' Claire announced on the first morning after they arrived home at Nardoo.

They were lingering over a late breakfast. Nancy and Joe Fiddler, their elderly caretakers, had insisted that they indulge in one last day of a slower routine before they launched back into full-scale station work.

Adam pushed his empty breakfast plate aside so he could sort through the huge pile of mail that had come while they'd been away. Now he looked up at her and smiled. 'Another garden? Sounds like a good idea.'

He knew that announcing a totally new project out of the blue was Claire's way of telling him she didn't want any more discussion about what had happened at Jim's.

Ever since the evening at her brother's, she'd looked vulnerable and uncertain. She'd spent the time in an agony of self-recrimination, going over and over how badly she'd behaved.

Now they were home, he could still see a haunting shadow dimming the loveliness in her eyes, but he hoped she would be able to put the whole regrettable incident behind her.

Claire always worried so much about what her family thought of her. Half the time he wondered why she bothered. Over the years, he'd had to hide his dismay when they hadn't been more concerned and supportive about her problems.

He remembered the disbelieving, reproachful expression on his mother-in-law's face when Claire had first tried to explain the difficulties she was having getting pregnant.

'I don't understand it,' Mary Tremaine had exclaimed with a petulant quiver in her voice. 'The women in our family never have trouble falling pregnant. Maybe you need to take more vitamins. Give some to Adam, too.'

Her younger sister, Sally, had been even less considerate than her mother. She'd simply grinned and winked at him as she'd commented flippantly, 'You can't really complain, Claire. Adam is so dishy that at least you can have a scrumptious time trying for a baby.'

And, of course, Jim and Maria had been so busy with their own family.

He noticed that, after initial attempts, Claire tended to avoid talking about her difficulties with her family. If they made enquiries, she invented cover-up lines. 'Every time I decide it's time to have a baby, Adam has to go off mustering,' she'd tell them with a laugh.

He slit another envelope open with his penknife and Claire picked up her teacup. He fancied there was a tinge too much enthusiasm in her voice as she said, 'I'm so glad it rained while we were away. I was worried that we'd come back to find everything in the garden brown and ugly.'

'You know Nancy and Joe wouldn't have let that happen. They've lived here for longer than I have and love it as much as we do. The place looks terrific.'

He pushed a pile of letters down the table towards her. 'These are yours.'

'I'll read them later.' She finished drinking her tea, replaced the cup on its saucer and stood. 'It was too dark to see everything last night. I want to check on all my babies.'

Jumping to his feet, he walked around the table till he stood beside her. He touched her soft, too pale cheek.

'Claire, you don't mind being buried out here in the outback, do you?'

'Oh, Adam,' she sighed, dropping her head onto his shoulder and rubbing her nose into his neck. He could smell the clean, sweet fragrance of her hair and the familiar soap they always used at home. 'Of course I don't mind. I love it here.' Then she kissed him and added, 'Besides, you're here.'

His heart gave a little tumble when he saw her innocent

smile, as if the simple fact of his presence was enough to keep her happy.

'I worry sometimes that being stuck in the bush makes everything harder for you. You've had to adjust to the isolation and you've been amazing the way you've learned so much about running the property. But you must miss your old friends. And you don't have children to keep you busy.'

'I've got the garden,' Claire insisted. 'And Heather Crowe has been onto me for years about taking part in the Open Garden Scheme. You know, opening our garden up to the public a couple of times each year. Apparently this district is getting quite famous for its gardens.'

'Would you like that?'

'I think I would. At least I'm going to give it some serious thought.' She kissed him again, lingeringly on the mouth. 'Now, please don't worry about me. I made a terrible mistake in Sydney, but it doesn't mean I'm becoming unhinged.'

'Another kiss like that and you'll never get to check your garden,' he told her with a sexy growl. 'Go, woman.'

Claire crossed the airy breakfast room and went down the hall, pausing to collect her hat from the row of akubras and oilskin coats in the entry-way, and then she stepped out through the heavy, silky oak-framed doorway onto the veranda where huge urns of lilies and wicker baskets full of lush ferns kept the front of the house looking cool and green all year round.

Before her stretched the Nardoo garden.

She was proud of the way she'd preserved the beautiful garden first planted by Adam's great-grandmother. And she was equally proud of the way she'd extended and developed it, without losing sight of the tone and vision of the original garden with its old-world plants, low stone walls and winding flagged paths.

Even though she'd grown up in Melbourne, from the minute she'd arrived at Nardoo as a young and hopeful bride Claire had loved Adam's home.

Last evening, as they'd rattled and bumped along the dirt track that led from the main road into their property, they'd both felt a kind of hushed awe as they'd looked around them at the enduring beauty of their own familiar, hazy bush and the soft silvery paddocks that ran down to the river.

Claire had felt the special thrill that only a true sense of belonging and homecoming could bring. She'd leant closer to Adam, slipped her hand along his jeans-clad thigh and rested her head against his shoulder.

And, without taking his eyes off the road, he'd half turned and kissed her forehead and said, 'Nothing quite like home, is there?'

'Absolutely nothing,' she'd agreed and she'd felt a flutter of hope that perhaps her shameful episode in Sydney could be allowed to slip away like a bad dream that faded in the forgiving light of morning.

Now she pulled her wide-brimmed hat down firmly over her blonde curls, walked out onto the expanse of rolling green lawn and turned to look back at the house. It was a gracious, low-set homestead built to house a big family in colonial times, featuring two magnificent bay windows at the front and a bull-nosed, wrap-around veranda.

Last year she'd supervised the house's repainting and, because she hadn't wanted it to look too new or bright, she'd chosen a weathered, dusty red for the iron roof and the soft blue-grey-green tone of the surrounding euca-lypts for the timber walls.

With its own separate nursery wing built in the late nineteenth century, it was a beautiful, welcoming house crying out for a family to fill it.

But Claire refused to let her mind linger on that dead-end path. She turned her attention to the familiar garden features.

One of her very special delights was to revisit her garden after a time away. There was always something new to discover. New shoots, new buds, and sometimes, sadly, the discovery that a struggling plant had succumbed to the heat, or that others had been eaten by wallabies.

So now, she revisited each part of her garden in turn. The jacarandas sweeping in a row away from one end of the house were still flowering and beneath them the lawn was covered by a romantic carpet of fallen lavender blue-bells.

The jasmine and bougainvillaea that rambled along the trellises on the veranda were still making a good show and her rose beds, filled with her favourite mixture of hybrid tea and David Austen roses, were a riot of colour.

She smiled. *Italy was grand, but it is most definitely good to be home.*

Stepping onto one of the rustic stone paths, she followed it past the hardy, summer stalwarts—pentas, zinnias and dahlias—around to the western side of the house where she wanted to plan a new garden. As she walked she brushed past lavender bushes and they welcomed her by giving up their fresh, heady perfume.

From this side of the house, she could see the flash of the river—the Maronoa—mighty in flood, but quiet and peaceful now. Wide and brown, the river was bordered by black-soil banks lined with century-old river gums.

Adam had told her once that during all the years he'd lived on Nardoo, the river had been like a favourite friend. And she'd understood exactly what he meant. Together, they'd spent many happy hours sitting and chatting, picnicking or fishing beside its wide, silky waters.

He'd built a rough stone barbecue up closer to the house in the shade of a row of ancient Moreton Bay fig trees. But from between the tree-trunks, they could still see the river and they'd enjoyed many outdoor meals there. Now she wanted to make the area into a proper courtyard to be lit at night by dainty fairy lights threaded through the tree branches.

She could picture a central pergola covered in yellow Banksian roses and perhaps a lily pond. And she wanted perfumed plants climbing over trellises to scent the evening air—hoya, port-wine magnolia and night-scented jasmine.

As Claire wandered further, planning happily, checking what other patches in the garden needed weeding or pruning or watering, she felt her garden begin to work its magic…soothing her and healing her hurt.

Restoring her faith in herself.

From the house, she heard the tinkle of the telephone, but she continued her inspection. Nancy would take the call.

The fresh tang of tomato plants reached her as she arrived at the raised vegetable gardens at the back of the house. Here, bok choy, tomatoes, parsnips and eggplants were planted alongside herbs for the kitchen—parsley, basil, oregano, mint and rosemary.

A garden fork was stuck in the earth and she picked it up and began to break up the soil. The ground gave up its moist, earthy scent and her nostrils twitched with pleasure.

She promised herself to put babies completely out of her mind, trusting that once she became absorbed in her garden again, she wouldn't feel so empty or downhearted.

It was ironic that she had a talent for winning fertility out of the earth when she...

No! No more negative thoughts.

She couldn't resist testing the rich chocolate texture of the freshly turned earth with her fingers and, almost immediately, she felt her spirits lift.

'Claire!' Nancy's voice reached her and she looked up to see their housekeeper standing on the back porch, holding the screen door open.

'Am I wanted on the telephone?' Claire called, annoyed, because she'd just started to get her hands dirty.

The housekeeper hurried towards her. 'You don't need to come, but your sister called,' she said as she drew closer.

'Sally? What does she want?'

Nancy grinned. 'She's staying in Daybreak and she's coming to visit you.'

'She's in Daybreak? Again?' Claire was genuinely surprised. Daybreak was the country town nearest to Nardoo, but Sally worked as a journalist in Brisbane and claimed to be an urban animal. In the past, she'd always shunned the bush. But over the past couple of years, Claire had noticed that her visits had been becoming more frequent.

'That explains why she didn't answer my call when I tried to ring her in Brisbane,' she told Nancy. 'I wonder what on earth has dragged her out here this time. Did she say when she's coming?'

'This evening.'

'Oh.' Claire realised as soon as it was out that her reply sounded less than enthusiastic. 'That's great,' she added with more energy. It wasn't that she wouldn't love to see Sally. There was never a dull second when her little sister was around.

But she couldn't help wondering if Sally had been in contact with Jim. Had she dashed out here to check on her? Her stomach churned at the thought. If Sally planned to cross-examine her, she could be in for an uncomfortable time.

CHAPTER FOUR

'I'VE been in contact with Jim.'

It wasn't the first thing Sally announced after she arrived that evening, but it came far too early in the conversation for Claire's comfort.

Shortly before sundown, Sally roared up to the front of the homestead in a hired truck. Claire met her with excited greetings and hugs and exclaimed over her sister's trendy new, short and spiky hair cut.

Sally's jaw dropped as she looked around her. 'My God, Claire, this garden is more amazing every time I see it. I've got to tell people about it when I go back. People who count. You should be on one of those television shows like *Burke's Backyard*.'

Before Claire could protest, Sally skipped to another topic, demanding full details about the trip to Italy, and while they talked they sat on the side veranda and sipped chilled white wine, listening to the parrots in the surrounding trees and watching the sun set behind the low hills beyond the river.

When Adam arrived, he welcomed Sally effusively and she, in turn, went through a flirting routine she seemed to reserve especially for her brother-in-law.

Eight years of marriage should have shown Claire there was absolutely no need for jealousy. All women went a little gaga over Adam. But even though she knew this and told herself not to be silly, her sister's antics always bothered her.

She hated to admit it, but she'd *always* been just a

47

little jealous of Sally. It was an emotion that had dogged her since she was seven years old when her mother had come home from hospital with her new baby sister.

At first she had been consumed with love for the sweet little doll-like baby girl, but when Sally had grown into a winsome child, clever and pretty and extrovert, Claire, who had been reserved and rather serious, had felt outshone by this bright, sunny little sister.

An unwilling resentment she hadn't dared admit to had lurked through the rest of her growing-up years.

Until she'd met Adam. Then, suddenly, she'd had someone wonderful—someone who loved her madly—someone her sister could never have.

As the sisters watched Adam head off to the cold room to select prime fillet steaks to cook on the barbecue, Claire grabbed the chance to ask Sally the question she'd been dying to ask all day. 'What's a metropolitan newspaper journalist with the famous Sally Tremaine byline doing out here in a remote country town like Daybreak?'

Sally, who was always very precise and specific about *everything*, suddenly became waffly and vague. 'Oh...' she murmured, and she fiddled with a trio of silver hoops in her earlobe. 'I persuaded our Chief of Staff that the paper needed some more rural colour...'

Sally seemed to be avoiding Claire's gaze, but she made a point of watching Adam as he returned to the barbecue and began to chop wood.

The action of wood-chopping seemed to maximise his masculine grace, showing off the breadth of his shoulders, the fluid strength in his arms and back, and the lean athleticism of his hips and legs.

'You do realise that husband of yours is stop-and-stare gorgeous, don't you?' Sally commented.

Claire couldn't help snapping, 'It's about time you found your own man to stop-and-stare at.'

'Ouch. Keep your claws in.' Sally laughed. 'I'm not planning to steal Adam. Just letting you know what a lucky gal you are.'

The truth was that Claire doubted if anyone realised just how intensely she fancied her husband. Sometimes the power of her feelings frightened her just a little.

'I have noticed he has one or two good points,' she answered with a wry smile.

But her smile faded when her sister switched subjects yet again and said, without any warning, 'I need to talk to you, Claire. I've been in contact with Jim. He told me about the offer you made—for Rosa.'

Claire's glass slipped from her hand and, to her utter dismay, it fell with a splintering crash onto the wooden veranda. She'd been mentally preparing for this all day, but it still caught her unawares.

Confused and embarrassed, she jumped up quickly, muttering, 'I'd better get a dustpan,' and, without looking at Sally, hurried off to the kitchen.

How stupid was that?

Her teeth ground together as she opened the cupboard beneath the sink and snatched up the dustpan and brush. How on earth could she try to minimise the episode at Jim's after a stupidly dramatic performance like smashing that glass?

Sally would jump to all sorts of conclusions about her emotional state! Wrong conclusions.

Her sister's words echoed in her head. *The offer you made.* Coming from Sally, it sounded even worse than she'd feared—as if she'd tried to bid for her brother's baby, without any emotion, the way Adam might bid for a bull at the sale yards.

It seemed there was no way she could hope to win her family's sympathy or understanding. They either thought she was desperate and unhinged or they decided she was unfeeling and greedy.

Returning to the veranda, she tried to look composed as she swept up the glass fragments. Sally didn't comment. She remained silently in her seat and smoked a cigarette while she watched her sister.

Claire wished Sally would say something. The thoughtful, considering light in her eyes unnerved her.

At last there was nothing left to be swept. She took the pan back to the kitchen, fetched another wineglass, lingered to check that the delicious salads Nancy had prepared weren't wilting in the heat and, although she still hadn't worked out what she would say to Sally, she went back outside to face her sister's relentless curiosity.

But Sally's chair was empty. She was talking to Adam.

Claire stood there for a moment, watching them, trying to calm her jumpy nerves. After spending all day in the garden, she'd been feeling tired but happy, the kind of happiness that came from physical effort, sunshine and a sense of achievement. Now she willed that calm mood to return.

Adam looked completely relaxed. He was standing at the barbecue with his back to her, but she could tell by the loose set of his shoulders that he was enjoying chatting with her sister.

Sally looked tiny beside him. She was shorter than Claire but had the same fine bone structure and similar deep brown eyes and fair hair. Now, with her hair cropped so short, the height of her cheekbones and the size of her eyes were accentuated. She was a startlingly attractive young woman.

As Claire watched, Sally and Adam leaned close towards each other. Sally was telling him something humorous. She could tell he was enjoying it by the way his shoulders shook as if he was holding in laughter. Suddenly, the joke must have reached its punchline.

A loud guffaw burst from Adam and he almost doubled over with mirth, holding his middle. Sally was giggling too, and she placed a hand lightly on his shoulder as they shared a moment of helpless hilarity.

Claire told herself she was silly to still feel jealous after all these years. This was how it always was with Sally. Ever since she was little, she'd been the live wire. She was the life of any gathering and she was also the wild child of the Tremaine family.

She had enjoyed a string of boyfriends and affairs and she'd left a trail of broken hearts scattered all over Brisbane and Sydney.

And yet, to Claire's knowledge, her little sister had never fallen in love.

Stepping off the veranda, she crossed the short stretch of grass to join them at the barbecue. The laughter died. There was a moment of noticeable silence. Great—not only was she considered a nut case, but she was a wet blanket, too.

'Steaks almost done?' she asked with forced brightness.

'Sure,' Adam said, turning quickly back to the fire to give the meat a final flip.

'I'll bring the salads out, then,' she told them. 'Everyone happy to eat on the veranda?'

The replies came in unison. 'Of course.'

'Perfect.'

Sally followed her. 'Let me give you a hand.'

While they ate their superbly tender steaks and crisp, tasty salads and drank a hearty South Australian red, the three of them resumed polite, friendly conversation. They found innocuous subjects to discuss such as the editorial direction of Sally's newspaper and more memories of the trip to Italy.

From the river, they could hear a baritone chorus of frogs. Adam cocked his ear in that direction. 'There's rain around,' he said.

Sally squinted at the starry sky beyond the veranda. 'There's no sign of rain—not a cloud in sight.'

'There'll be clouds *and* rain by tomorrow morning,' Adam assured her.

'You reckon?'

Claire smiled at her sister. 'If Adam says it's going to rain, believe me, it'll rain.'

One of Sally's eyebrows rose sceptically and Claire laughed. 'Adam's very in tune with the land. There are some things he just *knows*.'

Sally looked at her brother-in-law, her expression a mixture of doubt and grudging admiration. 'So the land shares its secrets with you, Adam?'

'Maybe,' he said with a slow smile.

After they'd eaten, Adam answered a phone call in his study and the two sisters retired into the lounge to have coffee. Claire had filled a tall glass vase with long stems of flowering ginger and the exotic scent lingered on the warm night air.

She slipped an Ella Fitzgerald CD into the player and a song floated around them like a bewitching, sentimental dream-cloud, while they drank their coffee and sampled a fine liqueur Adam had bought in Rome.

Kicking off her shoes, Sally tucked her feet under her and she curled onto the well-padded armchair like a contented kitten.

'Ah, my darling sister, the newspapers have got it all

wrong. It's just an urban myth that you guys have it tough in the outback.' She raised her glass to salute the elegantly furnished room with its soft wool carpets, beautiful paintings and heirloom silverware on gleaming antique side tables.

'A lot of people are having a terribly tough time,' Claire replied quickly. She felt compelled to add defensively, 'But there are two good reasons why we haven't suffered as badly as some. Firstly, this holding is very big, so it can weather the ups and downs of the market more easily, but also, Adam has diversified and made some very astute investments.'

'Can I quote you on that?'

'Don't you dare.'

Sally laughed. Then she drained her coffee cup and cocked her head to one side as she studied Claire. 'Tell me honestly. Do you really like living out here?'

'I love it,' Claire assured her.

'You don't ever get lonely or frightened?'

Claire sat a little straighter. 'Is this question motivated by sisterly concern or a journalistic need for a story?'

Sally leant forward, and her eyes softened. 'I worry about you. I find it hard to imagine what it's like to be stuck out here. You're so isolated. I don't know if I could handle it.'

Claire studied her sister's face and was surprised to see what looked like a sincere desire to understand. Heck! Why should she keep shielding her family from the truth? Why had she always gone to so much effort to assure them that her life was a bed of roses?

'There are times when I'm frightened,' she admitted carefully, 'but I'm sure I dwell on the dangers in the outback more than I should—more than Adam does.'

Placing her cup and saucer on a side table, she went

on less hesitantly, 'Sometimes when Adam's late back from a day in the bush, I sit here and drive myself nuts. While I wait, I try to convince myself that he's dealing with some kind of practical problem. He's repairing a pump, or changing a tyre, or his horse is lame. But I often have to fight off the feeling that the outback takes as easily as it gives.'

As Sally watched her carefully, she went on. 'I try not to think the worst, but it's hard sometimes not to wonder if he's fallen from a windmill tower, or if he's pinned underneath his vehicle in a washed-out creek or been bitten by a king brown snake. All those things have happened to various friends or neighbours of ours.'

Sally didn't speak. She just sat there, chewing her lower lip thoughtfully.

'So, while we're very comfortable,' Claire continued, 'there is always an edge of danger in our lives. I never feel isolated when I'm with Adam, but when he goes, the darker side of the bush seems to intrude somehow.'

She didn't add: So that's why I focus so intensely on my garden. That's why children would be such welcome company.

'If it's any comfort,' she heard Sally say with a heavy sigh, 'I don't know that there's any perfect place to live. The city can have its dark side, too, you know. *Homo metropolis* isn't the happiest species on the planet. You can be surrounded by people and still feel very lonely…if they're not the *right* people.'

Claire frowned as she saw a fleeting, but unmistakable sadness darken her sister's face. She wanted to ask some questions of her own. There seemed to be more to Sally's visit to Daybreak than she was prepared to admit. But before she could speak, Adam returned to join them.

But perhaps his mind had been running on similar

lines. As he helped himself to coffee and liqueur, his curious gaze rested on Sally. 'Did you run into Jack in town?'

'Jack?' she echoed and Claire watched in amazement as bright pink splashes of colour bloomed in her sister's cheeks. She'd never seen Sally blush before.

'Jack Townsend, my brother,' Adam elaborated dryly. 'You met him at our wedding but I know you've seen him since then. He's set up a veterinary practice in Daybreak.'

'Yes,' Sally admitted after the slightest hesitation. 'I did run into him, but he was dashing off to inseminate some poor, unsuspecting cows.' Her eyes danced wickedly as she added, '*Artificial* insemination, of course.'

And then, as if she wanted to get off the subject of Jack Townsend in a dreadful hurry, she rushed on to say, 'But then you two know all about IVF.'

And there it was again.

That subject.

To Claire it seemed to hang in the air like a guillotine, threatening to descend and spoil the evening. Ella Fitzgerald could sing as sexily as she liked, but the mood was spoiled completely.

She looked towards Adam and found that his eyes were already watching her. His dark brows drew together in the slightest of frowns. He was probably worried that she would disgrace herself in front of yet another family member.

Uncurling her legs, Sally sat straight in her chair. She looked from Claire to Adam. 'Look, you guys,' she said softly. 'I had no idea things were getting so bad for you.'

'What do you mean by that?' Adam asked.

Sally's face pulled into an embarrassed smile. 'Jim told

me about Claire's offer for their new baby.' She turned to Claire. 'I never realised you were so desperate.'

Claire's heartbeats stumbled. 'We're not desperate. I—I just thought, or rather I didn't think...'

'Hmm.' Sally looked unimpressed. She fiddled again with her earrings. 'Excuse me for being nosy, but have you two been told you definitely can't have kids?'

'No,' replied Adam vehemently.

Sally's eyes widened and she stared at him for a long moment, then she looked towards Claire.

'No one can tell us what the problem is,' Claire admitted.

'What a bummer!' Sally thumped the arm of her chair. 'I know I should have paid more attention to this ages ago, but I felt you didn't want to talk about it.'

With a shaky finger, Claire traced a pattern in the upholstery. 'It's not a very cheerful subject.'

'But I'd like to know now,' Sally insisted. 'Believe it or not, I really care about you guys. What have you tried? I take it you're not interested in adoption?'

'It's not that we're not interested,' Claire said defensively. 'It's more that we didn't feel we'd reached that point, yet. There aren't a lot of babies available these days and, somehow, lining up for adoption felt like we'd given up on ever hoping to have our own baby.'

Sally nodded. 'So, have you had all the tests? There are some pretty clued-up white coats in the big smoke, you know.'

Claire rolled her eyes. 'I've lost count of the number of trips we've had south in recent years. Just because we live in the bush and find getting to the clinics a major hassle doesn't mean we haven't tried.'

'Mum mentioned you'd had some tests, but I never knew the details.'

'We've tried everything. I've had a laparoscopy. Adam's had a sperm count.'

Sally grinned. 'I'd be surprised if he doesn't have the full complement of happy little swimmers.'

Claire caught Adam's eye and they shared a quick smile. 'He has squillions,' she reassured Sally. 'We've even had horrible post coital tests to make sure our juices are compatible.'

'That sounds choice.' Sally squirmed in her seat. 'And what about IVF?'

'We've tried one cycle of that, too, but it didn't work and we don't know if it's worth the trouble to try again.'

Adam added, 'We have to time it between musters so that we can spend big chunks of time in the city. That's always difficult.'

'So you've gone to all that trouble and there's still no result?'

Claire shook her head.

'There's no hope?'

'No one has said that,' Adam countered. 'The doctors have called it non-specific infertility.'

'So, in other words, they haven't got a flaming clue.'

'That's exactly it.' Claire sighed. 'I think it would have been easier if a problem had actually been uncovered.' Her old enemy, *tears*, began to line up in her eyes once more. However, this was one time when she definitely didn't want to get soppy.

Adam, bless him, must have sensed her edginess. He rose and crossed the room and stood behind her chair. She felt his big hands begin to massage her shoulders gently.

Dropping her head to one side, she rubbed her cheek against his forearm. What a dear, wonderful man he was.

She could feel the strength of his muscles against her

soft skin. How supremely lucky she was to have her husband's love. Adam was her rock. She kissed the warm skin on the back of his hand.

'I'm so sorry,' she heard Sally say in a low voice just above a whisper. 'I really mean it when I say that I wish there was something I could do.'

She heard Adam's deep laugh. 'That's a nice thought, little sister, but it's our problem. Claire and I are on our own with this one.'

'Maybe not.'

Claire had closed her eyes, but when she heard those words and felt Adam's hands grow still she shot them open again and discovered that Sally had risen to her feet. She was standing in front of them and her eyes burned with bright intensity.

Claire recognised that determined light. She had seen it in Jim's eyes last week when he'd torn up her cheque. She was quite certain she'd looked like that herself on several decisive occasions.

'What do you mean, Sally?'

'If nothing's working… If you've been trying for all these years and no one can help you…and you're getting desperate enough to want to buy someone else's baby…maybe…maybe I could help.'

For several seconds, Claire was sure that her heart stopped beating. She was aware of Adam's hands drifting away from her shoulders as she stared at her sister.

'Maybe I could have a baby for you,' Sally said.

CHAPTER FIVE

ADAM saw the deadly earnest expression on Sally's face and it was only with great difficulty that he suppressed the sudden desire to laugh outright at her suggestion. She wasn't joking!

She was standing there looking like a kid just out of high school in her bare feet and with her boyish haircut, dressed in a skimpy miniskirt and top. And she was offering to have a baby for them.

He wasn't sure how long he stood behind Claire's chair. He knew his jaw had dropped and he was gaping at Sally, but for the life of him he didn't know what to say. Claire also seemed to be experiencing difficulty coming up with a response.

Sally's eyes widened and she looked embarrassed while they both stared at her like dummies, stunned to silence.

The top right-hand corner of her mouth lifted into an uneasy smile. 'You guys are making me nervous,' she said. 'So what do you reckon? Good idea? Bad idea?'

'It's—it's an amazing idea,' said Claire eventually.

'It's a big idea to take on board in a hurry,' admitted Adam.

As life returned to his limbs, he lowered himself onto the arm of Claire's chair and she quickly slipped her hand into his. Bolstered by the reassurance of her warm fingers sandwiched within his grasp, he frowned at Sally.

'You're offering to have a baby. Forgive me for sounding thick, but I can't get my head around the details of how this would happen.'

Sally pulled her mouth into a tightly pursed smile. 'That's more or less up to you two.' Then, to Adam's surprise, she flopped back into an armchair and sat with her legs crossed and eyed them expectantly.

'So you want us to come up with a grand plan for you to conceive and produce a baby—for *us*?'

Directing her gaze at Claire, Sally said, 'One thing you'd need to decide is whether you'd settle for just any baby—that is, *any* father—or whether you'd like it to be Adam's baby.'

It was as if an invisible hand came out of the blue and hit him. Adam's head pounded. He almost fell off the chair. Dimly, he was aware that Claire was looking up at him with big, emotion-filled eyes. Her hand in his felt suddenly cold.

'*My* baby?' he managed to croak. 'You've got to be joking.'

'I wasn't joking, actually,' Sally said in a tight little voice. She shook her head and flung her hands away from her with a gesture of impatience. 'I'm not suggesting that I'd make a baby with you the old-fashioned way.' Then, with a knowing little Sally-style smirk, she added, 'More's the pity.'

Adam gulped and felt his ears redden. He avoided catching Claire's eye.

'All you would have to do is give me a—a deposit and I can do the rest with a turkey baster.'

'*A turkey baster!*' A picture of a Christmas turkey sizzling and dripping in a roasting pan floated into his imagination.

'Happens quite often,' Sally said. 'It's not all that different from what vets do with the animals. The baster functions like a syringe. And it works. Lots of people are into do-it-yourself surrogacy these days. I have gay friends who had a baby that way.'

'Hold on!' roared Adam. Then he realised he was shouting and dropped his voice. 'This is very—very—well, I guess it's very generous of you, Sal. But we're not your gay friends. I don't think Claire and I are quite ready for this kind of off-the-wall thinking.'

She shrugged. 'Of course, we could do it under clinical supervision if we go to the city.' After a pause, she added, 'There's no rush. There's a lot for you to think about.'

'There's a lot for you to consider, too,' said Claire.

Adam turned swiftly and shot an anxious glance towards his wife. She was leaning forward and looking very worked up. Tinges of colour underlined her cheekbones.

God help him! She looked and sounded as if she was seriously considering Sally's outrageous proposition.

'Have you really thought about whether you want to go through nine months of pregnancy…a labour…and then just hand your baby over?' Claire asked.

'I haven't been thinking about much else for the past twenty-four hours. I've decided it would be an interesting experience.'

'An interesting experience?' Adam repeated, shocked by her flippancy.

Sally's face broke into a grin. 'I'm a writer,' she added, as if that explained everything. 'All new experiences help to fill my creative well.' Then she looked at Claire again and her face softened. 'But, seriously, I'd really love to see my big sister with a baby in her arms.'

A kind of choked cry broke from Claire and in a moment she was across the room and the two sisters were clasping each other and their cheeks were silvered with tears.

Adam felt his own throat grow raw and painful. Hell! *What is happening?*

He stepped into the centre of the room and circled around the women awkwardly, terrified by the way they were clinging to each other as if they'd already clinched the deal. He felt as distanced as he had when Claire had tried to buy Rosa.

'We need to have a good, hard think about this,' he said loudly.

They didn't seem to hear him.

He tried again. 'It's not something you'd want to rush into.'

Claire looked at him over Sally's shoulder. Her eyes glowed damply. 'I know that, Adam, but it's so sweet of Sally to offer.'

'Yeah, sure.'

He scratched his head, wondering how the hell he could handle this situation. He tried to recall other times he'd been thrown by the unexpected. But all he could think of was the occasions he'd been thrown from a bucking bull in a rodeo, or from a horse when it had been startled by stampeding cattle. And he'd been more or less prepared for those dramas.

That kind of danger came with the territory. It was part and parcel of living and working in the outback.

But there was no way he could have anticipated Sally's little incendiary. The aftershocks were still vibrating through him.

At last the sisters broke apart.

Sally made a point of examining her oversized wristwatch and yawning loudly. 'I've been up since the crack of dawn. How about we all sleep on this?'

'Great idea,' Adam replied with perhaps a little more enthusiasm than was necessary.

Claire nodded and almost immediately she slipped her arm around her sister's shoulders and escorted her to one of the guest rooms. Adam turned off the CD player, gathered up the coffee-cups and liqueur glasses and took them through to the kitchen.

Claire had already loaded and switched on the dishwasher, so he piled the things carefully in the sink and ran hot water over them.

The house and the surrounding bush seemed unnaturally quiet.

Snapping off the tap, he stood listening for the reassuring, familiar sounds of the bush at night: the soft whinny of a horse in a nearby paddock, the call of an owl or a curlew, or the howl of a distant dingo. But the only sounds he could hear were the low, mechanical hum of the dishwasher and Claire's footsteps heading straight past the kitchen and down the hall to their bedroom.

Spidery tendrils of uneasiness prickled his stomach.

The carved sandalwood chest had stood beneath the bay window in Claire and Adam's bedroom for the past five years.

Kneeling beside it, Claire lifted the lid. She knew by heart every item it held, but she wanted to take one more peek at the beautiful linen she'd collected over the years while she'd dreamed of decorating a nursery.

There were rose-embroidered pillow cases, an ice-blue fringed woollen blanket, gingham sheets in pink, blue and lemon, an embroidered lavender bag to keep everything smelling fresh and a sage lace organza pillow to rest on her wicker rocking-chair.

She'd even slipped a little teddy bear and a collection

of Beatrix Potter books into the box. Each time she'd bought one of these items, she'd thought, This will be the month I'll fall pregnant.

The chest held so many precious hopes, so many exquisite dreams, and month after disappointing month she'd had to put them all on hold.

But now, with Sally's incredibly generous offer whispering to her over and over, she couldn't help feeling those dreams bubbling to life again.

She could picture the bedroom next to theirs transformed into a pretty nursery, beautifully decorated with all these lovely things.

And she could see a tiny baby. Perhaps a dear little girl like Rosa. In her mind's eye, she saw herself bending over a cot and making soothing noises as she scooped the baby into her arms.

The little darling would snuggle into her neck, just as Rosa had...and Claire would be able to comfort her, sing lullabies to her...rock her to sleep.

She stood there entranced as her imagination fleshed out her dreams, adding colour and movement... She could see herself stooping to switch on a cute little rabbit-shaped night-light.

She could almost smell the fresh, sweet baby powder...and hear little baby sounds...a happy chuckle...the tiny cry of a little voice...needing her...

She would be such a good mother. She would be patient and understanding. She would—

'Claire.'

Dropping the lid, she swung around, startled. She hadn't heard Adam come into the room.

'A penny for your thoughts,' he said as he took her hands in his and drew her to her feet. For a moment he looked down at her, his deep blue eyes searching her face.

He smiled in that sleepy, sexy way of his that always made her go soft and warm inside. 'Hang on, I have a better idea,' he murmured and he rested a hand at her nape and tilted her head back slightly. 'Don't tell me what you've been thinking until I've kissed you.' Without a moment's delay, he lowered his mouth over hers.

Claire was already smiling as Adam's parted lips met her upturned face, but the relaxed smile quickly trembled into a deeper, hotter yearning as he traced his mouth slowly back and forth over her lips, teasing her. Pausing to taste her.

Tempting her.

And she could never resist his temptations. Especially not tonight when her emotions were as keen as a finely tuned violin.

Slipping her arms around his neck, she pulled him closer, urging him to deepen the kiss, to feed a desperate need inside her. And he responded with a soft groan as his tongue delved and tangled hotly with hers.

Oh, yes! This was exactly what she needed. Her husband was like deep, rich, fertile soil. She could put her roots down and grow in him.

She'd always cherished the strong cradle of his arms. She never tired of the familiar, exciting taste of him. And right now she feasted on the swirl of purely physical pleasure that licked through her as his strong, supple body urged hard against hers.

She needed her man. Needed him to fill her emptiness. And there was a feverish darkness in Adam's eyes that told Claire his hunger matched hers.

No need for words. They could read each other too

well. Their clothes fell about them on the carpet as, between greedy kisses, they stumbled towards the bed.

So many times, they'd made love in the past, and in so many moods, but tonight it was different again. Tonight there was an edge of darkness mingled with their longing.

Claire wasn't sure where it had sprung from, but she could feel it in herself and in Adam, like a pulsing, tangible force. It heightened their tension, deepened their passion.

She wondered if couples about to be parted by war made love as they did tonight. With a kind of desperation. As if they were staking a claim. As if they couldn't know what tomorrow held, but, chances were, it would be bad. As if the only way to ward off fear of the unknown was this intensely intimate coupling.

Afterwards they lay together, both a little shaken by what had happened. Claire rested her head on Adam's shoulder and he ran gentle, caressing fingers through her hair. For a long time they were silent, while their heartbeats subsided and their minds adjusted.

After some time, Adam rolled sideways and nuzzled her shoulder. 'You know I love you very, very much,' he said. 'You're the sweetest, prettiest girl on the block.'

Claire smiled. His words were like a cool breeze at the end of a blistering summer's day. This was their private joke and it brought relief from the tension that still lingered. Apart from sixty-year-old Nancy, Claire was the *only* girl on the block—all ten thousand square kilometres of it.

'You know I love you, too,' she murmured against his neck.

His hand slowly traced the line of her backbone.

'When I came into the room earlier…you were looking at that box…you were thinking about a baby.'

She nodded against his shoulder.

'Sally's baby?'

'I was imagining it here. I could see it here with us.'

A deep sigh shuddered through him.

Claire raised her head. 'Don't you want a baby?'

'Of course I want a baby. You know that, Claire.' She sensed there was more he wanted to say but he was searching for the right words. 'But I would prefer a baby that's a—a reflection of you—someone who comes from us and our love. I'm not sure that I want Sally's baby.'

Without warning, a fierce reaction exploded and zapped through her. She tried to hold back the thundering wave of disappointment but it broke over her, shattering her dreams and filling her with dark panic.

Sitting up in bed, she clutched the sheet around her and wriggled away from Adam. Surely he wasn't going to spoil this beautiful opportunity?

She had to make him understand what a wonderful chance Sally offered.

'Sally would only be the birth mother,' she hurried to explain. 'Once the baby was born, it would be mine. I mean ours. It will be *our* baby—especially if you're the father.'

Adam sat up, too. 'And you could live with the idea of mixing my seed with your sister's?'

For a ghastly moment, she stared at him. The baby would be his and Sally's. Adam's sperm, Sally's egg combining to make a new life. Nothing of hers. Could she handle that? 'I—I wouldn't think about it that way.'

His jaw tensed. 'So how would you think about it?'

'I'd concentrate on the result rather than the process.' Why did this have to be so difficult? She'd been given a chance to have the baby she yearned for. No other woman was likely to make such a generous offer. It really was very sweet of Sally.

Claire needed space to think. She edged even further away till she reached the foot of the bed. '*You* think about it, Adam. If ever there was a case where the end justifies the means, this has to be it.'

They sat facing each other down the length of the big white bed.

'I'm sorry,' Adam said, 'but I'm very uncomfortable with this idea. It just doesn't feel right.'

She made an effort to sound conciliatory. 'I know it's a shock, but I think we'll get used to it.'

He shook his head slowly. 'I certainly don't think we should make any rushed decisions.'

Claire felt another surge of helpless panic. 'We're hardly rushing,' she cried. 'We've been waiting for five years.' She leaned towards him, pleading, gripping the brass knob at the foot of the bed. 'How much longer do you want to wait? If we say yes to Sally now, we could be parents by the end of next year. Think about how wonderful Christmas would be if we had a baby.'

'Christmas?' he repeated and he looked puzzled and worried. '*Christmas?* Now you're getting sentimental. We've got to keep our heads about this.'

'For crying out loud, Adam, how can I help being sentimental? This is an emotional situation. Can't you see? Wanting a baby is like—it's like falling in love. Once the feeling grabs you, you can't do anything about it.'

Suddenly deflated, Claire flopped forward onto the bed and blinked. She refused to give into any more tears.

Adam bent forward and reached out his suntanned hand to close it over hers. 'Sweetheart, that's OK as long as the emotion is shared.'

Frightened, she looked up at him as she whispered, 'What are you saying?'

'I'm afraid that in this situation, my emotional response doesn't match yours. I can't get excited about this. I'm not particularly interested in supplying your sister with the ingredients to fill up her creative well.'

'Oh, for pity's sake! You know Sally was joking about that! She always hides her real feelings behind jokes.'

'Maybe she does, but if this baby is the product of my sperm, a flaming turkey baster and your kid sister, then the only emotion I feel is—is—completely negative.'

She snatched her hand away. If only Adam wouldn't keep harping on the process! Of course it wasn't a very appealing concept. 'Surely there's a positive way to look at this,' she said less certainly.

He didn't answer.

She clung to the vision she'd seen...of the baby's room...a tiny, pink and white baby in her arms... Her own baby. Surely they should seize this chance?

She pushed herself upright once more. 'Adam, I think you're being selfish.'

'*I'm* being selfish?' He sounded so shocked it was almost comical.

'Yes. This is the one thing I want more than anything else and you won't cooperate.'

His face darkened. 'You know I'd do anything to make you happy.'

'Obviously not.' Claire's lip trembled as she looked away.

After a long, ghastly silence, he asked, 'You really want a turkey-baster baby?'

'*Stop calling it that!*'

'I'm just trying to get a little reality into this discussion.'

She punched the mattress with her clenched fist. 'You're just trying to kill the most important dream I've ever had!'

He stared at her for a painful moment and then his shoulders sagged and his head fell forward as he released another weary sigh. 'I think Sally's right,' he said. 'We should sleep on this and perhaps things will make more sense in the morning.'

Without looking at her or saying another word, he stood up and walked away from her.

Claire watched his retreating back. *Oh, God!* This was awful. Adam had never looked at her with such a closed-in, hard and angry expression. And he'd never walked away from her in the middle of a conversation before.

She heard the bathroom door click shut.

Why couldn't he understand?

Wrapped in numb misery, she sat huddled on the bed while she listened to him turning on the shower.

Fighting with Adam felt unbelievably bad.

Already she was beginning to feel ashamed of the way she'd behaved. She shouldn't have accused him of self-ishness.

The past few years had been hard for him, too. He'd been disappointed. She knew that. But throughout the whole time, he'd remained optimistic and had been prepared to try anything she'd asked.

He'd been incredibly *un*selfish.

Many times, it had been very difficult for him to get away from the property to be involved in medical procedures in the city, but he'd always done his best to co-operate. And, despite all the intrusive testing, he'd always kept his sense of humour and found ways to keep their sex life spicy and fun.

The only time he'd ever balked at any baby-making plan was tonight when he'd heard Sally's proposal.

It's all very well for me to say forget about the process and concentrate on the result, but I wouldn't have to be involved in this process.

Adam would.

And the baby would be his and Sally's...

That was the hitch. And she had to admit it was a major hitch. But if she wanted a baby, she had to keep pushing her mind past that.

She was still sitting on the bed, wrestling with her thoughts, when she heard the taps turn off again. She listened to Adam opening and closing cupboard doors and cleaning his teeth. When he came back to bed, she looked up. 'I'm sorry,' she said. 'You're not selfish, Adam. I should never have said that.'

To her dismay, he didn't reply.

He simply climbed into bed and lay on his back, staring at the ceiling with his hands linked behind his head. Claire could sense the bristling tension in his body.

She tried once more to reach him. 'Can we finish talking about this?'

'I said I'd prefer to leave the matter for now.'

Shocked, she hurried into the bathroom, but when she got into bed Adam still didn't look her way. They lay side by side, each locked in a cold and solid silence.

Claire felt wretched. She had pushed Adam to the point where they couldn't talk about this any more. If they tried, they would probably start arguing again. Over and over, round and round in circles. Never meeting.

They'd had tiffs before, but nothing like this. It was frightening that they could love each other so deeply and yet find themselves fighting so heatedly.

And now they were left with this coldly, horrible tension.

Unable to bear the sight of him looking so hard and unyielding, she rolled away from him as far as she could and gripped her pillow as she stared across the room at the sandalwood chest.

'We should sleep on this,' he'd said. She couldn't imagine that sleep would help. How could their situation be any different in the morning?

For the first time in their eight years of marriage, they turned out their bedside lamps without exchanging any parting words. There were none of the usual smiles or touches.

And no goodnight kiss.

During the early hours, Claire woke from a muddled dream about babies in Christmas stockings to find Adam's space in the bed beside her empty.

She was so used to snuggling against him when she woke that she sat up, suddenly alarmed. His side of the bed was quite cold.

Her eyes darted to the door of their *ensuite* bathroom, but she couldn't see a chink of light showing beneath it.

She wondered if he'd gone to close some windows. Perhaps, as he'd predicted last night, there was a storm coming. Listening carefully, she sniffed the pre-dawn air for a hint of rain. But there was no smell of dampening dust, no distant rumble of thunder and no sudden gust of wind through the treetops as rain approached.

Curious and worried, she slipped out of bed and padded barefoot to the doorway. She peered down the hall. No light in the kitchen. The whole house seemed to be in darkness.

She needed to talk to Adam, to apologise for being so obsessive last night and to tell him she understood how he felt. It was important to talk to him again before they saw Sally.

She hauled on jeans and a tee shirt. This was the time Adam always got up, so perhaps he'd just risen earlier than usual.

Full of her mission to make amends, she walked towards the kitchen and her nose twitched as she smelled coffee brewing. Then she heard lowered voices. A sharp pang of disquiet skittered through her and she hurried forward.

Through the big kitchen window, she could see that the first glimmer of morning was lightening the sky. And then, in the half-dark, she saw Sally and Adam sitting at the table, leaning towards each other and talking in intense, hushed tones.

She froze in the shadowy hallway.

How long had these two been sitting here whispering in the dark?

Adam was dressed in his work clothes—jeans, a blue-checked cotton shirt and riding boots.

Sally was still in her nightie—a tiny scrap of violet silk with shoestring straps. She was leaning forward, one hand propping her forehead, the other wrapped around a coffee-mug.

The nightie's straps had slipped from her shoulders and from where Claire stood she caught an eyeful of the feminine, smoothly rounded tops of her sister's breasts.

What was going on? Sally was never out of bed at this hour!

Adam never drank coffee first thing in the morning. Claire always made him a big pot of tea, hot and strong, the way he liked it. Her hands shook. She closed them into fists against her thighs and told herself she was overreacting.

This liaison was innocent. Of course it was.

She took a tiny, hesitant step forward and Adam swung around.

'Claire!'

She didn't feel any better when he looked shocked by her sudden appearance.

'Good morning.' Her voice was barely above a whisper.

'Hi, sis,' said Sally sleepily.

'Since when have you been an early bird?' Claire couldn't help asking.

'I'm not. This is torture.' Sally groaned theatrically and pulled the coffee-mug towards her, hugging it against her chest. 'But I have to get back to Brisbane today and I need to drop into Daybreak again on the way, so I'll have to push off soon.'

Questions buzzed in Claire's head. What had they been discussing? Why hadn't Sally mentioned an early rise last night?

In a daze, she wandered across the room to the electric kettle and switched it on.

'Sally and I have been talking about her suggestion and—er—going over a few details,' Adam said.

'You could have waited for me,' Claire snapped. Her good intentions dissolved as she felt anger and her old jealousy rising hotly through her. Grabbing a mug from the cupboard, she thumped it down on the kitchen bench.

Seeing Adam and Sally together…talking in secret…excluding her… Suddenly she wondered if there was another question she should have asked last night. Just why was her little sister so keen to have Adam's baby?

Every jealous cell in her body jumped to attention.

How on earth could she have thought Sally's proposal

was a wonderful idea last night? If Adam and Sally made a baby together, no matter what method they used, the baby would be *theirs*. She might get to feed it and care for it, but till the end of time Adam and Sally would be its biological parents and share a special bond.

Their relationship would go way beyond the normal brother-in-law–sister-in-law scenario.

And she would always feel like this. She would always be the outsider. The jealous outsider.

Sally's solution was no better than her own embarrassing attempt to acquire baby Rosa.

The kettle came to the boil, bubbled and then stopped. Claire ignored it.

She stepped towards the table. 'You don't need to discuss the baby deal any further,' she said.

Two pairs of disbelieving eyes turned her way and she almost caved in. Was she making a terrible mistake? Whatever she said now could mean the end of her most cherished dream.

Her reluctant gaze settled once more on the generous swell of Sally's breasts. Poorly disguised by thin violet-coloured silk, they were poised rather conveniently at Adam's eye level. How dared her sister flaunt herself like that?

Claire's chin lifted defiantly. 'I've been thinking it over, Sally, and thanks very much for your very kind offer, but I don't think it suits us at the moment.'

Sally's big brown eyes, so like her own, widened. 'Really?' She shot a puzzled, private glance Adam's way. 'I thought—'

'It seemed like a great idea at first,' Claire hurried on to explain. 'But Adam's not comfortable and—'

There was another ambiguous, silent exchange between Adam and Sally and Claire's heart tripped. She stared at Adam. What *had* these two been saying?

'You said last night you didn't like the idea,' she reminded him.

'And you said how badly you want this baby.'

'But I've had more time to think about it.'

'I see. You must have done quite a lot of thinking to have changed your mind so definitely.'

'I have.'

He looked pensively at his empty coffee cup for a lengthy moment and then shrugged. Finally he looked up at Claire uncertainly. 'So you're quite sure you don't want this baby?'

She pulled out a chair and sat down quickly before her shaking knees gave way. Was she sure? This could be her last chance. She might be saying goodbye to the only chance she'd ever have for a baby of her own.

But the reality was that it wouldn't be her own. It would be *theirs*. 'I'm sure,' she whispered.

Sally looked distinctly unhappy. Her bottom lip pouted obstinately. 'I really thought this pregnancy would help you out.'

Claire felt a momentary pang of sympathy. She'd thought she was helping Jim and Maria out. Maybe her family always got their wires crossed.

There was a sudden, loud thunderclap overhead and it was as if the heavens opened and an avalanche of rain pelted the iron roof above them.

Sally's eyes widened and she looked at Adam. 'You were right. It's jolly well raining.' Then she drooped once more and sighed loudly as she looked back to Claire. 'Are you absolutely sure about this? I had myself all psyched up to have a baby.'

Claire felt suddenly very sure and clear-headed. 'There's nothing to stop you having a baby if you want one, Sally,' she said loudly above the noisy drumming of the rain. 'It just won't be Adam's.'

CHAPTER SIX

'HAPPY New Year.'

Legs entwined, Adam and Claire lay naked, their bodies damp with summer heat and the aftermath of their lovemaking.

'A *very* Happy New Year,' Claire murmured as she nestled her head on his shoulder and watched the moon reach through the bay window to cast interesting patterns of light and shade on their bodies—making their torsos and legs look pale and sculpted—like marble works of art.

She squinted at the clock on their bedside table. It was one a.m. on January first. Turning back to Adam, she nuzzled his collar-bone. 'This is going to be the best year yet.'

His splayed hand settled on her waist and, with a slow, possessive action, he traced the upward curve from her waist to her hip. 'We've already made the best possible start.'

'Yeah.' Claire grinned. 'And I've a short-list of resolutions for the rest of the year and I mean to keep every one.'

He chuckled. 'So we're going to make love like that every night?'

Smiling, she leaned closer and nibbled at the underside of his jaw and the lobe of his ear. 'You're on the right track,' she told him. 'I'm certainly planning to think positively.'

'About?'

'About my life. Constructive thinking.' She pushed herself up on one elbow, so she could look Adam in the eye. 'There's one thing I can definitely promise. I'm going to avoid a four letter word that begins with b and ends with y!'

'You think that's the way to go?' he asked softly and his hand reached automatically to stroke her arm as if he felt the need to keep her calm.

'Absolutely,' she said and patted his hand to reassure him that she didn't need soothing. She was perfectly calm about this. 'I know I've been making life miserable for both of us. It's time to move on. I want to live in the moment. I'm going to build that new courtyard and I think I'd like to try my hand at more entertaining. Have more people here for dinners and parties.'

'You did a great job at Christmas.'

'Yes, I enjoyed it. It was good to have Jack join us, too. We don't see enough of him. I like your little brother.' She smiled up at Adam. 'You know, he's almost as handsome as you and just as charming.'

'*Almost* as charming.'

'Adam, you're jealous.'

'Too right.'

'OK—Jack's almost as nice as you are,' she said with a grin. 'But actually, I must admit, he can be a bit gruff at times.'

'How do you mean?'

'When I asked him about Sally's visit to Daybreak just before Christmas, he became very taciturn.'

Adam laughed. 'That sister of yours is likely to make most fellows think twice before they speak.'

'I suppose so,' she agreed. 'Anyhow, speaking of families, part of my New Year's plan is to look at things the way your family does.'

'Really? In what way?'

'Well, they've survived in the outback by working in with nature, rather than against it.'

Adam nodded and drew her back to snuggle against him.

'I've been thinking about it quite a bit,' she continued with her cheek pressed to the reassuring wall of his chest. 'Outback people know that when the floods come you can take your stock to high ground, but you can't try to hold back the water. And they know you can cut fire-breaks, but, even so, every five to ten years the whole country will be swept by fires. They trust that after the fires, the pasture will be rejuvenated.'

Dropping a kiss on her forehead, he yawned. 'You're being very philosophical for this time in the morning.'

'Bear with me,' she chided gently. 'I've nearly finished. What I'm saying is, you've got to endure the leaner years so you can be there for the good times.'

'And the good times will come, Claire.'

'I know. I know they will.'

'So go to sleep now.'

Only a few days into January, the wet season arrived with a vengeance and it stayed in the Maranoa district for the whole of January and February. Adam watched the river rise, and the billabongs fill and overflow, but to his relief the stretch of river below Nardoo didn't break its banks.

Hundreds of birds gathered along the waterways. One afternoon he came home to tell Claire he'd seen terns that had flown all the way inland from the ocean to fish in the rich floodwaters.

With so much rain, work couldn't start on Claire's courtyard, but, nevertheless, she started planning and designing. Adam knew she was very talented. Chances were if she'd stayed in the city, she'd have had a successful landscape gardening business by now.

His wife had given up more than she ever admitted when she'd married him, but she was so loyal and gutsy she never spoke about it. Just the same, the knowledge weighed heavily on Adam. But he began to relax as he saw how happy she was these days.

This new project brought dancing lights sparkling in her eyes. Each evening her face glowed with genuine excitement as she showed him the progress she'd made with her plans.

It wasn't until her birthday rolled around in March that Claire found it difficult to keep negative thoughts from creeping in.

She knew she should be feeling on top of the world. Adam bought her the most beautiful earrings for her birthday. Teardrop pearls set with garnets from Mt. Surprise.

She did her best to hide from him the fact that she was feeling a bit down, but it was hard to keep things from Nancy.

'What's the matter with you?' the housekeeper asked, when she found Claire in the kitchen looking morbid.

'Oh, Nance, I'm just being silly and female and starting to worry about my age. The old biological clock and all that.'

'Lord, dearie,' Nancy scoffed. 'It's too early for you to worry about that. Why, you're not as old as Adam and he's only turning thirty-five this year.'

'Men like Adam just get more distinguished-looking and gorgeous each year.' *And they can stay fertile till they're almost geriatric!*

Claire was about to let out a tired sigh when suddenly

she beamed at Nancy. 'Thirty-five! You've just given me the best idea. I'm getting better at playing hostess and I'm going to give Adam a big slap-up party for his birthday in October.'

'Thirty-five is something of a landmark year,' Nancy agreed. 'That would be nice. Real nice.'

'We have stacks of time to plan it.'

'And you've got the work started on your new courtyard and the pergolas. They should be looking beautiful by then.'

'Yes,' said Claire, picking up a notepad, eager to start making notes. 'Yes. It's a great idea.'

At Easter, Claire and Adam were invited to Rosa's christening in Sydney, but as the mustering had already started it was too difficult for them to get away. Claire was helping the mustering team and they were away from the homestead for several weeks. When they got back, they discovered that Maria had sent them photos.

'Little Rosa looks very sweet in the clothes you bought in Italy,' Adam said as Claire passed him the photos.

'I wonder if I've been forgiven?' she asked and he saw the sudden wary darkness that shadowed her beautiful face.

'I'm sure everyone has put it behind them,' he assured her.

He wanted very much for her to believe him. She had to believe him. It was unhealthy for her to go on feeling bad about that incident for ever.

Autumn progressed and brought milder, kinder weather. It was the time of the year when Claire worked harder than ever in her garden. Joe helped her to spread many barrow-loads of manure and hay for mulching.

By June, her roses and vegetables were flourishing so well that when she was approached again about opening her garden to the public, she agreed to have it registered as part of the Open Garden Scheme.

'Not only can I share my garden with others,' Claire told Adam, 'but I can propagate plants that do well in this district and sell the seedlings and the cuttings I've struck.'

She thrust typescripted pages into his hand. 'I thought I could make a little brochure with some of my gardening tips as well. "Tips for Bush Gardening" or "Beautiful Bush Gardens"—something like that. What do you think?'

He pulled her in close and kissed her just below her ear and murmured, 'How about "Beautiful Bush Gardener"?'

Claire loved living in the outback in winter. The mornings were so crisp and clear and the skies were cloudless and a brittle, vivid blue.

Although she'd finished helping with the mustering, she liked to go down to the stockyards and sit on the sliprails to watch Adam and Joe drafting stock into the yards.

If Adam saw her there, he tended to show off and she loved it. It was rather delicious to watch her man and his horse working together, leaping sideways after an escaping beast, the two of them turning fluidly like choreographed dancers.

He rode his favourite horse, Flashman, an Australian stock horse descended from the line his forebears had bred when they'd first arrived on Nardoo. She knew that Adam's grandfather had ridden one of Flashman's ancestors with the Lighthorse Brigade in World War One.

But thinking about the long history of Adam's family on this property made her desperately sad. There might not be another generation of Townsends...

But that was forbidden territory!

She didn't hear from Sally at all. Adam tried to reassure her that it wasn't unusual. Sally was always very casual. She would turn up again—out of the blue—taking them completely by surprise.

But she was concerned that her sister hadn't replied to any of her letters or that whenever she rang she could only get the answering machine. Her mother and Jim were vague about Sally, too, but she got the distinct impression that at least they had heard from her.

They fobbed her off with comments about Sally being fine and that her job at the paper kept her incredibly busy.

Claire was busy, too, and the months slipped by so easily that she was surprised to realise it was September already. Only a month till Adam's birthday!

She began to feel a little nervous. She'd had several successful dinner parties during the year but hosting a big function would be very different. Nevertheless this party was something she really wanted to do for Adam.

The invitations went out and replies came back with pleasing promptness. People were coming from all over the district.

What really amazed her was that she managed to keep the party a surprise. She thanked heavens for Nancy! They arranged for the mail to be delivered to her and Joe's cottage, so they could take out the replies before the rest of the mail was sent up to the big house. Adam didn't have any suspicions.

When it came to planning the catering, Nancy was a huge help there, too. She and Claire settled on the menu for the buffet dinner—cold seafood salad, shallot and artichoke tarts, braised veal shanks, lovely, big legs of lamb marinated in fresh rosemary, thyme and red wine.

Nancy offered to make her special pear bread puddings for dessert and her nieces volunteered to come in from Daybreak to give them a hand on the day of the party.

The best part about so much busyness was that it helped Claire to realise what she'd always known deep down. There were many ways to be happy and fulfilled without being a mother.

She felt she'd learned a great deal about herself in the past nine months.

CHAPTER SEVEN

WHAT was that?

Foggy with sleep, Adam's head shot up from his pillow as he tried to make sense of the noises he was sure he'd heard outside.

He was certain a vehicle had just come to a screeching halt at the front of the house.

Yes! As he listened his ears caught the distinctive squeak of a car door opening.

Frowning, he swung out of bed and in two strides crossed the room. He pulled the curtain aside and peered through the pre-dawn murkiness in the direction of the sound, but the angle of the house blocked his view.

Just then he heard a second squeak—another car door opening. He glanced towards the bed and spared a quick half-smile for Claire, who was still sound asleep, sprawled on her back with one arm flung over her face.

Grabbing his jeans from a nearby chair, he hurried out of the bedroom, dragging them on as he went.

But he'd only made it halfway down the hall when he heard car doors slamming shut again and an engine roaring to life once more. There was a blast of exhaust like a rocket being launched to the moon. He raced to the front door and dragged it open.

Too late.

A dusty utility truck was already disappearing down the track leading away from Nardoo. Adam had a brief glimpse of its rear lights before they were swallowed up by the avenue of she oaks.

He stood on the veranda, staring after it, scratching his bare chest in a bleary-eyed, half-asleep daze. What the blue blazes was going on?

He looked up and down the veranda to see if the caller had left anything and blinked suddenly. He'd almost missed it at first, but there was a bulky, dark shape behind one of the thick timber supports near the front steps.

It was a curious, unrecognisable shape. Frowning, he edged cautiously towards it. If one of his neighbours had dropped something off, he might have expected to find a pile of papers, a jerrycan, or perhaps a wooden barrel or a crate. Two steps closer and his heart was thumping. *'Struth!* There was something alive. It moved.

He took another step.

Then he hunkered down closer, his throat dry with apprehension. It was too shadowy to see intricate details, but he could recognise the starfish shape of a tiny human hand waving in front of him.

A baby.

Stuff this for a joke.

As his eyes adjusted to the thin light of early dawn, Adam peered more closely and made out the outlines of a baby capsule—the kind people used to transport infants in cars—and a carry bag beside it. And there was a piece of paper pinned to one of the bag's plastic handles.

Suddenly the little form in the capsule let out a dreadful wail. A loud, gut-wrenching, pitiful cry. And Adam's stomach sank.

Bloody hell!

Reaching out a tentative hand, he patted the little round bundle. He could feel a soft wool blanket and something small and squirming beneath it. 'Hey,' he whispered. 'Take it easy, mate.'

The wails grew louder.

Desperate, Adam shot a pleading glance across the lawn to the spot where the front driveway disappeared into the trees. Maybe, by some miracle, the driver would realise there'd been a dreadful mistake and at any minute the truck would come racing back down the track to reclaim this abandoned child.

But he didn't like the chances.

The baby's cries were getting louder. They bordered on ear-splitting now.

He was marshalling the courage to pick the kid up when a cool hand touched his bare shoulder.

'Adam, what on earth's going on?'

He turned and gaped at Claire. Dressed in a striped cotton dressing gown, she was standing behind him, her nut-brown eyes huge in her pale face. For a minute he thought she might faint, she looked so pale and shocked.

He swallowed. 'It's a baby.'

'I kind of gathered that, but what's it doing here?' she whispered.

'I'm not feeling too bright at the moment, but my guess is someone's dumped it.'

The baby screamed and Adam shot a helpless look Claire's way. He felt more at home facing a charging bull than a shrieking baby.

'The poor little thing!' She swooped forward and picked it up. Within seconds, she was holding a little blue bundle against her shoulder, jigging it with little up-and-down motions and making shushing sounds.

She kissed its cheek and murmured softly, 'There, there. Hush, don't cry. You'll be all right.'

To Adam's relief, after she'd paced up and down for a minute or two, the screams began to subside and eventually they quietened into subdued hiccups.

'Thank heavens one of us knows what to do,' he murmured.

A triumphant light shone in Claire's eyes as she looked at him and said, 'What a darling, good little baby.' She glanced at the capsule and bag. 'I guess we should take all this stuff inside and see what we can find out.'

As soon as they reached the kitchen, Adam turned the light on and scanned the note. A wave of shock blasted through him. 'Hell,' he muttered.

'What?'

'It's Sally's.'

Claire frowned. 'What's Sally's?' Then, after a gasp of disbelief, she added, 'Not the baby?'

'Yeah. That's what this note says. This is your sister's kid.'

'Read it to me,' Claire ordered, her voice suddenly sharp with tension.

But Adam was already halfway across the kitchen, heading for the car keys hanging on the hook near the stove. 'I'm going after her,' he muttered. 'She won't have driven very far and this is flaming ridiculous. She can't do this to us.'

'Adam!' cried Claire. 'You can't just race off after my sister and leave me like this!'

He paused in mid-stride and looked back at Claire and his heart plunged like a duck full of gunshot. She was clutching the baby to her chest as if she was terrified it would be snatched away at any minute. Her eyes were wide with panic.

A painful flash of insight descended. Where were his brains?

A baby had arrived at Nardoo. A baby for Claire. A longed-for, cherished dream come true. Apparently...her sister's gift.

Whoa, there, Adam. Time to think. This moment presented a deeply emotional crisis for his wife.

Hands on hips, he stood in the middle of the kitchen, and stared at the timber floorboards, while his mind spun. If he dashed after Sally Tremaine and demanded that she take the baby back, he would be responding on a very simplistic level to a deeply complicated situation.

Chances were he'd have two angry women on his hands!

'Please tell me what the letter says,' Claire urged.

'Of course.' He opened the crumpled paper in his hand and began to read.

'Dear Claire and Adam,
Here he is. My little gift to you. I've called him Rosco. I hope you like the name. He was born on September the fifth.'

Adam looked across at Claire and shook his head. 'He's only three weeks old!' he said. 'It's ridiculous! Crazy!'

'Keep reading!' she said tightly.

He cleared his throat.

'I'm so thrilled to be able to give you the baby you've longed for, Claire. I know you will love him and be a wonderful mother. And Adam, belated Happy Father's Day.'

He let out an impatient groan before reading on.

'Clothes, formula and everything else Rosco needs for the first few weeks are in the bag. After that, I'm sure you'll work out what you need.

I love you guys. That's why I did it.
Your loving sister,
Sally.
P.S. Don't try to find me. I'm going to be out of contact for a while. Once the shock wears off, you'll be fine.'

When he finished reading, Claire stared at him. It was some time before she spoke. 'I can't believe she did it,' she whispered finally. 'Sally had a baby for me.'

'Who would have thought she'd damn well go ahead with a madcap scheme like that?'

'I thought we told her not to bother.'

'She can't have been listening too hard.'

'She didn't even tell me she was pregnant. All this time and *no one* told me.'

Claire grabbed the back of a chair with a shaking hand and, holding the baby against her, she lowered herself into it.

'Your family aren't the best communicators and they're so spread out—Brisbane, Sydney, Melbourne,' Adam reminded her gently. 'Besides, they probably thought it might upset you.'

Claire looked down at the little boy in her arms. 'Sally must have fallen pregnant the very minute she left here.'

'Yeah.'

She attempted a smile, but failed.

The unspoken thought hung in the air between them. Another of Claire's relatives was as fertile as a field mouse.

'At least the little guy's stopped crying,' he said, deciding it was time to direct attention back to the baby. 'Rosco's a weird name, isn't it?'

Claire's chin lifted to a stubborn angle. 'I think it's lovely. It's—it's a unique name. It's very Sally and it's rather dignified.'

'Yeah, of course. Rosco Tremaine...or Rosco Townsend. Either way it sounds fine.'

His tension lessened momentarily as he saw the way her big brown eyes grew misty and soft as she took a good long look at the tiny bundle in her arms.

'I can't believe it,' she said softly. 'The doctors always told us that if we put babies out of our minds, one might turn up unexpectedly, but I bet they never guessed it would happen this way.'

'This wasn't how I pictured it either.'

After a few more minutes of gazing at the little fellow, she said, 'Come and say hello to our little boy, Adam. He's so *cute*!'

'Don't get carried away, sweetheart. I'm going to do my best to track Sally down. There's no way we can just assume this baby's ours to keep until we've had a proper talk to her.'

Claire rolled her eyes. 'You read the letter, Adam, and I know my sister. She won't go back on her word. And she won't let us find her till she's ready to be found.'

'Maybe, but I'm not so sure we shouldn't make a determined effort to find her anyhow. She's left us with far too many unanswered questions. I like everything to be clear-cut. I want more details.'

'What sort of details?'

'Well, for starters, if you and I are to be this baby's parents, I'd like to know how we can adopt him officially.'

'I'm sure we'll sort all that out with Sally later.'

'And I'd be very interested in sighting a birth certificate.'

She frowned. 'Why? Don't you believe Sally is his mother?'

'It's not that,' Adam said quickly. Then he sighed noisily. What he really wanted to know was why Sally was hiding. It bothered him that there seemed to be aspects of this birth that she didn't want to reveal.

Like the identity of the baby's father.

'Come over here, Adam,' Claire said quickly, looking worried, as if she was afraid that he would start rejecting the whole idea of keeping the baby. 'It won't hurt you to take a proper look at Rosco.'

Stepping forward, he took up a position of relative safety just behind Claire. From there, he could peer over her shoulder at the tiny creature. He was used to newborn animals, but the only times he'd been at close quarters with a baby human there had usually been an entire gaggle of females providing a comforting barrier between himself and the infant.

This tiny fellow was scowling at the end of his own nose and sucking his fist noisily.

'He looks a bit cross-eyed,' Adam said.

'All new babies look like that,' Claire scoffed. 'Their eyes have to learn to focus properly.' She dropped a kiss on the little boy's fat cheek. 'I think he's just gorgeous.'

'At least he has a good head of hair.'

Claire stroked the dark, downy cap of hair. 'It's lovely. Like yours. As a matter of fact, Adam—' Cocking her head to one side, she looked over her shoulder at him and studied his features. Then she looked at the baby again.

Her smile wavered.

Adam frowned. 'What's the matter?'

'He looks like you.'

'You're kidding. I don't look anything like that.'

'You did when you were a few weeks old. I've seen photos.'

Adam shrugged. 'Most little babies look much the same, don't they?'

'You could be his father.'

'Claire!' Blood rushed into his face. 'You're talking absolute rubbish.'

'OK, Adam,' she said softly, but she continued to stare at him with a thoughtful frown. 'Don't burst a blood vessel. You're right. I know you couldn't possibly be his father.'

The flash of panic in Adam's guts subsided. Almost.

Claire nuzzled the back of the baby's neck. 'Why don't you make us a cup of tea while I find out what we have in this bag to feed our little guy.'

As Adam rattled about the kitchen, he called over his shoulder, 'What about all the gear you're supposed to have for babies? We're going to need something for him to sleep in, aren't we? He wouldn't want to spend all his time in that little capsule.'

Claire looked surprised. 'That's not a problem. Don't you remember that room at the end of the nursery wing? The one that's locked up. It's chock a block with baby gear.'

'Really? I wouldn't have a clue what's there. Haven't been near that room for years.'

'Well, I know there's a bassinet and a bath. They're pretty old, but I'm sure with a bit of a clean-up they'll do for the time being.'

'That's handy. Straight after breakfast, we'd better check it out.'

* * *

As good as his word, Adam found the baby equipment and helped Claire to dust and clean it before he headed off on horseback to work up the river with a contract fencer.

Reassuring him that she would be fine and that, with Nancy's help, she would manage the baby beautifully, she waved him goodbye and then mixed Rosco's milk according to the instructions on the tin. Bubbling with excitement, she settled herself in her rocking-chair to feed him.

Rosco's brow furrowed with concentration and his dark little eyes stared straight up at her with a very serious expression as he sucked. If Claire hadn't already loved him, she fell in love with him then.

Afterwards, full of milk, he snuggled contentedly against her with his little head resting on her shoulder. His feather-soft breath came in tiny puffs against her neck and a completely new level of happiness began to seep through her.

She sat very still and savoured the way his trusting little body grew floppy and relaxed in her arms, like a bow coming undone. Soon he was asleep.

When she was quite sure he was sound asleep, she gently lowered him onto her lap so she could take a good long look at her baby.

Her baby.

A baby of my own.

Thinking of that brought her first giddy stirrings of mother love—the poignant, sweet thrill of knowing that at last she was to be a mother. This tiny little person would grow up needing her completely, loving her without question.

She was his *mother*!

What a wonderful gift he was!

Her sister's gift. She'd given them a baby after all and without having to involve Adam.

Tears blurred her vision as she thought about Sally. It was so hard to imagine this warm little baby growing inside Sal for nine long months.

She tried to picture her sister's body becoming round and heavily pregnant. And what about Rosco's birth? Had it been difficult? Sally was so finely built and Rosco was such a bonny, bouncing boy.

And, after all *that*, how could Sally bear to give him up now?

She had been *so* generous. Suddenly Claire wanted her sister to be there. Wanted to wrap her arms around her and to thank her. Thank her for being so sweet, so clever and so very big-hearted.

But it was then, when she pictured Sally rocketing back up to the house, that she also imagined her suddenly announcing that she'd changed her mind and would like her baby back. The image brought a sharp, unexpected slam of panic.

And it returned to haunt Claire throughout the day.

One minute she would be excitedly planning the finer details of Rosco's room, the next she would be fighting off pangs of guilt, thoughts that she shouldn't really keep him. 'Sally would just tell me to take a chill pill—a whole bottle of them,' she told the sleeping baby with a fond smile. Of course everything would be all right. This was what Sally wanted for her.

But as the day wore on, guilty doubts began to linger with annoying persistence until they lodged deep inside her like an unavoidable pain.

Rosco *wasn't* hers.

When Nancy, usually so unflappable and brimming with good old-fashioned common sense, arrived at the homestead to start vacuuming carpets, her reaction didn't help Claire at all.

'Good heavens,' she repeated over and over. 'I'm too old for shocks like this, Claire. I've come over all dizzy.' And she had to sit down for a full fifteen minutes.

Claire made her a cup of tea.

'Adam and I were rather shocked, too,' she admitted.

'That little sister of yours. Who would have thought?'

'Well, she did mention the idea when she was here last December, but we thought we'd talked her out of it.'

'Last December?' Nancy repeated. 'That's nine months ago.'

'Yes. It looks as if Sally didn't waste any time.'

Nancy chewed her bottom lip thoughtfully. 'You're going to have your hands full, looking after this little fellow plus all the preparations you have planned for Adam's party.'

'I'll manage.'

'*We'll* manage,' Nancy said with a reassuring smile. And then she frowned again and pushed herself up out of the chair before crossing the room to take a closer look at the sleeping baby.

Claire followed nervously, not at all happy with the dark, mysterious air Nancy had adopted. She stood beside the housekeeper and looked down at Rosco, innocently asleep in the old family bassinet.

'He's an absolute darling, isn't he?'

'He's very handsome,' Nancy agreed.

'The first thing I noticed was his dark hair,' Claire said. 'But look at his eyelashes. They're incredibly dark and long as well.'

As she stood next to Nancy she couldn't help admiring the baby all over again. She had lined the bassinet with a blue gingham sheet and he was lying with his head to one side and a tiny hand curled near his chubby cheek.

She was fascinated by the minute perfection of his little fingers, each topped by a fine, transparent fingernail.

As far as Claire was concerned, every tiny feature of Rosco was beautiful—his neat little ears, his nicely shaped nose and his dimpled chin.

Nancy's pale blue gaze settled shrewdly on Claire. 'Poppet, did Sally tell you who the father is?'

Something in Nancy's expression frightened Claire. Her heart began a painful kind of hammering. 'No,' she whispered. 'She only left a very brief note and she didn't mention anything about the father.'

Nancy's mouth pulled in tight as if she was holding back a comment.

'It doesn't really matter who the father is,' Claire said.

'I don't suppose so,' replied Nancy in a tone that implied the exact opposite.

Claire didn't want to ask, but she found the question slipping out anyhow. 'Did you have some special reason for asking?'

The housekeeper placed a work-worn hand on Claire's shoulder. 'Claire, honey, I don't want you to take this the wrong way, but I think you should be prepared for the fact that a lot of people will see a mighty strong resemblance between this little baby and your Adam.'

'Do you—?' Oh, God, she could hardly breathe. 'Do you really think so?'

'Oh, yes, dear. I remember Adam when he was born. He was such a bonny baby. See the dimple in Rosco's chin. Adam's was exactly the same. And the hair and the shape of the nose...'

Claire snatched her gaze away from the baby, and by some miracle, she forced her voice to sound light. 'I know there's a bit of a similarity. I've seen Adam's baby photos. But I'm sure any resemblance between him and—and my sister's baby is just a coincidence.'

'I'm sure it is, too, dear. All I'm saying is be prepared for tongues to wag. There are always some folk who can't keep their jaws from flapping.'

After Nancy turned on the vacuum cleaner and began her attack on the lounge carpet, Claire fled to the photo album that was stored in a cupboard in the study.

With shaking hands she leafed through the early pages which showed black and white wedding shots of Adam's parents, and then she arrived at his baby photos.

Oh, God, yes! The likeness was even stronger than she had remembered. Her heart slammed around in her chest as if it were being pummelled by a heavyweight boxer. The baby lying there in Adam's mother's arms could have been Rosco.

The evidence was unshakeable—just as Nancy had said—the same dark hair, the same shape of the nose and that dimpled cleft in the chin! Even on a tiny baby it was very distinctive.

Claire's mouth trembled and she pressed her fingers hard against her lips. Adam couldn't be the baby's father, she told herself. He couldn't.

There were no secrets in their marriage. He would have told her if he and Sally had gone ahead with the turkey baster idea.

And as for any other possibility…the thought was too absurd to contemplate. He wouldn't do *that*.

He didn't!

Sick and shaking, Claire shoved the album back into the cupboard and locked the door. The key was usually left in the lock, but today she walked to the big desk in the corner of the room and put it safely out of sight in the stationery drawer.

By the time Rosco woke for his mid-afternoon feed, Nancy had finished her housework and had gone back to her own cottage with a basket of tablecloths to iron in preparation for the party.

Alone with her tortuous thoughts, Claire set about preparing Rosco's next bottle, but she didn't enjoy the task nearly as much as she had that morning.

In the rocking-chair again, she offered him his milk and she tried to relax and enjoy the peaceful view of the garden. It was looking its spring best, but she couldn't admire it today. She couldn't stop thinking about that fateful morning last summer.

The morning Sally had left Nardoo. The morning she had woken to find Adam had left their bed.

A ghostly chill snaked down her spine and she shivered as she remembered that moment when she'd found them together in the kitchen.

Adam and Sally.

But she mustn't get carried away. Adam had simply been talking to Sally. Talking and drinking coffee! *That was all!*

Of course, they hadn't been...

Her hopeless imagination was racing out of control! Valiantly, she struggled to keep it in check.

The baby splurted and coughed.

'Oh, I'm sorry,' she told him. 'You poor little boy. The milk's been coming out too fast.' She lifted him to her shoulder and patted his back and tried to calm down.

But the memories and doubts persisted.

She kept thinking about the way her sister had always flirted with Adam. Ever since Claire had first taken him home, Sally had always raved about Adam's gorgeous looks.

OK. So Sally might have been interested, but it took two to tango.

And Adam… As she thought of the part Adam might have played in all this, her heart faltered scarily.

Her miserable thoughts were interrupted by baby Rosco grumbling restlessly against her shoulder and she remembered with a guilty start that she was supposed to be feeding him. Lowering him onto her lap again, she held the bottle to his mouth once more.

But he must have been picking up on her restless vibes. He didn't want any more milk. Instead of settling to feed, he arched his little back and pulled away from the teat, emitting a fierce yell of complaint.

And when Claire set the bottle aside and tried to soothe him by rocking and singing to him, his cries continued. Perhaps he had wind? She stood up and began to pace up and down, patting his back gently as she'd seen other mothers do.

Rosco continued to cry.

He was still crying an hour and a half later when Adam came home.

CHAPTER EIGHT

ADAM'S horse cantered at a slow and steady pace along the high river bank. As he drew closer to home his thoughts were full of Claire and the baby. And, for the most part, his thoughts were anxious.

He had bad vibes about this new turn their lives had taken. The arrival of a baby should be an occasion for celebration. But right now there seemed to be little to celebrate. There were too many questions. Too many doubts.

But, as he often did when he was troubled, he deliberately pushed the worries aside and turned his attention instead to the quiet beauty of his surroundings. A flock of black ducks swooped over his head and settled neatly one after the other on the flat surface of the sleepy river. Their landings were as precisely timed as jets coming into a busy airport.

Across the river above the far bank, a huge flock of budgerigars circled in a fluttering mass of green and gold flashes like pieces of foil paper tossed against the bright afternoon sky.

And as he neared the homestead he heard the noisy chatters and shrieks of sulphur-crested cockatoos gathering in the trees along the river as they did every afternoon.

With a rueful smile he acknowledged that even if his home life was a bit topsy-turvy, he could always count on the wildlife to behave predictably.

But after he'd stabled his horse and stepped onto the

veranda, he heard another less familiar sound—the pitiful wails of a baby. What kind of day had it been for Claire?

He dropped his muddy riding boots near the kitchen door and padded through the house in his thick woollen socks. It wasn't hard to track Claire down—simply a matter of following the sounds of the baby until he found her in their bedroom, pacing up and down the carpet.

He paused in the doorway, enjoying the novel sight of his wife in the role of mother.

She was walking slowly down the length of the generously sized room and she had her back to him. The baby's head was lying against her shoulder and there was something about the contrast of his little head with its straight black hair so close to her light golden curls that made Adam's throat constrict.

He knew he shouldn't be surprised by the sudden rush of tenderness he felt for Claire, but the sheer force of his feelings could still catch him out after all their years of marriage.

Was he imagining it or did she look more motherly already? Didn't her arms look a little softer and rounder as they encircled and rocked the baby?

He chuckled quietly as he watched the way she walked. There was no doubt that, beneath the soft blue fabric of her skirt, her slim hips were swaying. It was as if she was using her whole body in her effort to comfort the baby.

One thing was certain. Claire was incredibly sensuous. It was a very special gift of hers. Without doubt, she was a woman who knew how to use her body as an instrument of comfort. But he shouldn't be thinking about that now!

It was vitally important to track down her sister so they could sort this situation out as quickly and painlessly as possible. He wasn't at all happy with the furtive way

Sally had handed the baby over—as if she couldn't quite face up to what she was doing.

Everything about it was too tenuous, too unreal—like some sensational story she'd cooked up for that newspaper she wrote for.

Claire reached the far wall and turned, ready to pace back the other way. Adam stepped towards her and she looked up suddenly.

'Hi there, Mummy.'

'Adam!'

The wariness in her eyes froze the smile on his face.

He frowned. He'd been about to make a joke about the joys of motherhood, but the plaintive cries of the baby combined with her strained and closed-in expression made it seem like putting the boot in—kicking her when she was already down.

'What kind of day have you had?' he asked instead.

'Oh, I've had a ripper of a day,' she said through gritted teeth.

'That bad, eh?'

'Rosco's been crying for hours.'

Adam's stomach tightened.

There was something bothering Claire. Something beyond exhaustion. He knew her too well. She'd wanted a baby so badly and for so long. And she knew what babies were like. A few hours of crying wouldn't make her this upset.

She was deeply troubled.

His mind sprinted, trying to make sense of this. Of course, having the baby arrive out of the blue this morning had been quite a shock. Perhaps she was upset that her little sister had achieved so easily the very thing she had failed at.

But that wasn't a question he could ask her. If she did

feel any resentment about Sally's pregnancy, she wouldn't thank him for forcing her to admit it.

'Have you given him his tucker?' he asked her now.

She rolled her eyes towards the ceiling. 'Of course.'

That about emptied his repertoire of questions to ask about crying babies. 'Would you like a spell? I can take him for a bit.'

She hesitated and Adam felt a wave of relief. If Claire did hand the baby over, he didn't have a clue what he would do with him. He had a feeling he would be as effective as a mountain goat afraid of heights.

But suddenly she thrust the little warm bundle at him. 'I would appreciate a break. Here, you take him.'

And, next moment, he was fielding the surprising weight of little Rosco while he watched Claire hurry out of the room.

He wanted to rush after her, to find out what her problem was, but he didn't have time to dwell on Claire's mood with this squirming little shrieker taking centre stage.

'Left holding the baby,' he mused, holding Rosco tightly around the middle with both hands.

He had a job to get on with.

'Now, don't wriggle too much, little mate,' he warned. 'I'd hate to drop you.' Newborn animals he could handle. Baby humans were another kettle of fish altogether.

Gingerly, he held the stiff little body closer to his chest. The baby seemed to be pulling his legs up into his stomach. 'I think you have a pain in the gut,' Adam told him. 'You been guzzling your feed too fast? I've been known to do that on occasions. What you need is a walk. It's good for the digestion. How about I take you outside and show you around?'

Instinctively holding Rosco so that his stomach was

pressed firmly against his chest, Adam paced through the house, out to the veranda. As he went down the steps he did his manful best to ignore the baby's cries and he felt a pang of sympathy for Claire. Perhaps a screaming baby was enough to make her look so wrung out.

Claire sat at the kitchen table with her head in her hands and listened to Rosco's cries and Adam's footsteps as he made his way along the wooden veranda and down the steps.

Oh, heavens! She was a mess! When Adam had come into the bedroom just now and sent her one of his beautiful smiles, her knees had almost given way. She loved him so much. This was their first day as parents. She should be on top of the world.

But all afternoon her mind had been like a dog worrying a bone, going over and over the question of Rosco's father. When she'd seen Adam looking so dark and strong and drop-dead gorgeous, the pain of such thoughts had come back with a vengeance.

It was too much to cope with a crying baby and such tormenting thoughts all at once.

She thumped the kitchen table with a helpless fist. Surely Adam hadn't slept with Sally? It couldn't be true. She tried to force her mind elsewhere, but she still couldn't leave the problem alone.

Wild and vicious thoughts kept chasing each other back and forth.

You'd be sick in the head to start suspecting your husband. You know Adam wouldn't do that. Not ever.

How can you be so sure?

Because he's—he's Adam! To start with, he hardly paid any attention to Sally.

But he was ready to do anything to please you.

But he wouldn't do that. He couldn't make love to
Sally. He wouldn't go that far just for the sake of a baby.

Wouldn't he? Can't you remember how possessed you
were at the time? How you accused him of being selfish?
Adam would have done anything to please you.

No! No! No!

She'd wanted a baby for so long, but not at that price.
Never at that price.

What on earth was she going to do?

'Now listen, mate,' Adam said to Rosco as he stood in
the middle of Claire's new courtyard. 'This is Nardoo.
And it looks like it's going to be your home. You could
do a lot worse than end up here.'

Just talking about it sent his mind flashing back to his
own boyhood. He and Jack had spent their youth making
the most of the outdoors: canoeing and fishing on the
river, exploring the country—camping out under the
stars. He'd begun riding a horse at such a young age, he
couldn't remember how he'd learned—it was as if he'd
been born in the saddle.

'It's a terrific place for a kid—all kinds of animals,
plenty of open space and clean air, good tucker.' As
Adam paced he looked down towards the river. Lit rosy
pink and gold by the afternoon sun, it was slinking across
the landscape like a sleepy snake. 'You've got nothing
to complain about, young man.'

Suddenly, there was an explosion in the baby's lower
regions. Adam stopped his pacing.

And Rosco stopped crying.

'Was that the problem?' he asked softly, before glanc-
ing nervously over his shoulder towards the house.
'Claire?' he called. Then his pace quickened and an edge
of panic sharpened his voice. *'Claire?'*

Hurrying back up to the veranda, he called Claire a third time and, to his relief, she appeared at the kitchen door. 'I think the problem's solved,' he told her.

'Oh?' Her expression was careful.

'Well, partly solved,' he amended. 'He's stopped crying, but I think he's filled his jocks.'

He held the baby out to her, but she stood in the doorway with her arms crossed over her chest.

'You're going to help me out, aren't you, sweetheart? This is scary territory. After all, I'm only a bloke.'

The expected smile didn't happen. 'We should probably give him a bath,' she said. 'Bring him into the kitchen. I'll set up the baby bath on the table here.'

Leaning a bulky shoulder against a kitchen cupboard, Adam held Rosco and watched as she filled a plastic tub with warm water and tested the temperature with her elbow. She set out soft white bath towels and wash cloths, a tin of baby talc, a box of baby wipes and a little set of clean clothes.

'Where'd all that stuff come from?' he asked.

She blushed. 'I've had it tucked away in a cupboard for some time now.'

Again Adam felt uneasy. Claire had been wanting a baby for so many years—she'd had so many things ready and waiting for so long—but where was the excitement? The joy? There was definitely something wrong.

She took Rosco from him, laid him on a towel on the table and began to undress him. And, despite his concerns, Adam couldn't help but be fascinated as the mottled pink limbs and little body emerged. Before long the naked baby was lying there looking exactly as he should—like a pink and perfect miniature human being.

And he submitted to the attention Claire paid to his bottom with impressive, dignified silence.

'He's a grand little fellow,' Adam commented.

Claire nodded, but looked upset.

'Do you reckon he'd be slippery when he's wet and soapy?'

'There's a special way you have to hold them,' she told him and then proceeded to demonstrate by slipping her left arm behind Rosco's head and grasping his shoulder firmly. With her other hand she held his legs and lifted him carefully into the water.

Then she continued to support his upper body while letting his legs go.

'That's impressive,' Adam told her. 'I'd rather leg rope a steer than try to do that.' He was rewarded by the merest chink of a smile.

Rosco lay there quietly for a minute and both Claire and Adam watched him intently.

Adam said, 'I think he likes it.'

At the sudden sound of his voice, the little body jerked and Rosco frightened himself as he thrashed in the water. He cried again.

'Shh,' Claire murmured in a soothing manner and bent low and kissed the baby's cheek. He calmed quickly and began to give little kicks. With a tiny white face-washer, Claire drizzled warm water over his chest and then she began to bath him.

Briefly, she glanced towards Adam and he could see the flush of pleasure in her cheeks.

The tight knot in his stomach began to loosen. Maybe the effects of the bad day she'd had were wearing off.

'You're great at doing that,' he said. 'You're a natural at this mothering business.'

Her face was hidden by a tumble of curls so he couldn't see her reaction.

In silence, he watched her graceful movements as she

finished washing Rosco, lifted him out of the bath and wrapped him in a towel.

She looked up at Adam and, with a lurch of disappointment, he noticed her expression was still unsmiling as she asked, 'Would you mind emptying the bath water on the vegetable garden?'

Would you mind telling me what's bugging you?

With supreme will-power, he resisted the temptation to pose his own question. He sensed that, somehow, this wasn't the best time and place for a heart-to-heart discussion about what was troubling Claire.

So, mindful of the fact that no water was wasted in the outback, he carried the bath outside and almost bumped into Nancy as she came up the path carrying a casserole dish in her hand.

'Evening, Adam. I told Claire I'd cook a double batch of stew and bring you some,' she said. 'I know what it's like settling in with a new baby. It's hard to find leftover energy to get an evening meal for your husband.'

They stood facing each other awkwardly, Adam holding the bath and its water and Nancy a pottery casserole dish.

'Thanks, Nancy,' he said. 'Much appreciated.'

As he was about to step over to the vegetable patch, it occurred to him that Nancy could hold a clue to Claire's behaviour.

'I think Claire's had a tough day,' he commented.

Nancy's eyes narrowed. 'You'll put her mind at rest, won't you, lad?'

Her mind at rest? Adam knew he looked puzzled. Then the penny dropped. 'No need to worry, Nance. I've already reassured her she's a natural mother. Wonderful. She seems to know quite a lot about caring for a baby.'

'A natural mother?' Nancy repeated and her voice suggested that it was the most unsatisfactory answer she'd ever heard. She hesitated, as if she wanted to question Adam further, but then she must have thought better of it, because she turned and continued on into the house.

Puzzled, he carefully released the bath water in a steady stream between the rows of zucchini and returned to the kitchen to find the two women clucking over the clean and freshly dressed baby.

'He'll probably be hungry again by now,' Nancy was saying. 'Make sure he takes this next bottle nice and calmly and he'll no doubt sleep for hours. Must be exhausted, the poor little mite.'

She cast an uncertain glance over her shoulder in Adam's direction as if she suspected his very presence might turn the baby's formula sour.

Grabbing a beer from the fridge, he decided to leave the women to it. He'd had enough of mysteries. Retiring to the study, he headed straight for the telephone.

It was time for some answers. Time to track down Sally Tremaine.

CHAPTER NINE

AFTER she'd fed Rosco and put him to bed, Claire was surprised to find Adam at work in the study. He hadn't turned on the main light, so he was sitting at the old-fashioned silky oak desk, surrounded by gloomy twilight with only a little circle of yellow cast by the goose-neck desk lamp.

The telephone directory was open in front of him and he was leaning forward, running his finger down the finely printed lists of names. In the lamplight, his hair gleamed, dark as a crow's wing, and the back of his neck looked tanned and strong. Reliable.

On any other evening she might have bent low and kissed it, breathing in the scents he carried from the out-doors—sunshine and eucalyptus.

'The baby's asleep at last,' she told him.

He turned. 'You look tired, too.' His voice was gentle and he held out a hand to her. Oh, Lord! She wasn't prepared for the tender way he smiled at her. 'Come here,' he said. 'Take the weight off your feet.'

Normally, those words would have brought her curling onto his lap with her head tucked into the welcoming curve of his shoulder. But tonight Claire couldn't move forward. Instead, she stepped stiffly backwards, nearer the door.

'I'll put Nancy's casserole in the microwave and heat it through,' she mumbled.

'If you'd rather.'

She was aware of the cautious tone in his reply. He

didn't move, just remained seated at the desk, watching her, and she could sense his concerned gaze following her retreat to the kitchen.

She couldn't bear this! She hurried across the kitchen floor, snatched up the casserole dish and plonked it into the microwave, slammed the door shut and punched in the necessary digits.

Everything is too hard!

She had a newborn baby to care for. A huge party to plan. And yet hovering over all that was the fear that the baby's mother might come back at any minute and claim him as her own. And then there was the even bigger fear that her sickening jealousy was warranted.

That Adam could be the baby's father.

That he and Sally had made love.

Claire felt as if she were teetering on the edge of a very flat Earth. One wrong step and she would tumble into endless, empty nothingness.

If she were sensible and brave, she would put the fateful question to Adam. Clear the air once and for all.

It would be a simple matter to march straight back to the study, to open the drawer in the desk, find the key and pull out the photo album. She should confront him with the damning evidence.

In her head, she could hear her voice, challenging him. Tell me, Adam, are you Rosco's father?

That was all it would take. Four simple words. *Are you Rosco's father?*

And the answer was even more simple. Yes, no, or maybe. That was all. It would be over in seconds.

Then she would know one way or another. She would know if her husband had slept with her sister.

But she couldn't do it. She *couldn't*! She didn't dare. She was as helpless as a sprayed insect. It was too much to ask. Too scary. How could she face *that* awful possibility?

Standing at the sink, Claire clutched its edge for support and her hunched shoulders shook with the effort of holding back tears.

She heard Adam's footsteps as he came into the kitchen and then his startled exclamation, 'Claire!'

In two swift strides, he closed the gap between them and she felt his big hands settle on her quivering shoulders. He tried to draw her back against his chest, but she stiffened, almost flinched at his touch.

This was awful. She couldn't believe she was behaving this way with Adam. *Her* Adam. The man whose arms had always meant paradise for her—sweet comfort and perfect release.

For a tense, silent stretch of time, she sensed him standing there with his hands hovering uselessly in the highly charged air above her shoulders, then, eventually, she heard them slap as they fell against his thighs.

'What's the matter?' he asked in a voice so shaken she hardly recognised it as his. 'How can I help, Claire?'

She couldn't answer. If she opened her mouth, she knew nothing would come out except loud, heartbroken sobs. Or, worse, she might blurt out the dreaded question.

Behind them, the microwave pinged. Claire's stomach churned at the thought of food. She heard Adam's resigned sigh and his voice saying dully, 'So you're opting for the silent treatment. You know I don't play those kind of games. I'm going to eat. I'll set the table here in the kitchen tonight, so we'll be closer to the baby if he cries.'

She nodded and took a deep breath and forced herself to think about basic things the way he could. If Adam could think about their dinner and the baby, so could she. Any minute now she would begin to feel calmer.

But Adam didn't set about the routine domestic task he'd offered to do. He remained standing close behind her and the next minute he said softly, 'I've been trying to track down Sally.'

Panic raced through her. Spinning around, she cried desperately, 'Why?'

Her heart shuddered when she saw how suddenly pale and drawn Adam looked and the single word seemed to ring through the silent house, like a gunshot from a hidden sniper.

'*Why?*' he repeated, frowning. 'Because—because, damn it, we have to get some answers.'

'Do we?' She wrung her hands together, feeling so sick and scared she thought she might faint.

'Don't you want to know the full story about this baby? Isn't not knowing what's making you so upset?'

'I—I—guess so.'

'You guess so?' With an arm raised, rubbing the back of his neck, he stood staring at her. 'Well,' he said after some time, 'there are things I certainly want answered. I want to know if Sally plans to let us adopt Rosco. You know—officially. Then we'll know exactly where we stand.'

Adoption... 'Is that all you want to know?'

'It's a start, isn't it?'

'Yes,' she said faintly. 'Yes, of course.'

His mouth twisted as he forced a smile. 'Taking on a baby isn't quite the same as acquiring a poddy calf. We can't just slap a branding iron on the poor little fellow and claim him as ours.'

'No,' Claire whispered. 'Of course not.'

She waited for Adam to continue with the list of questions he wanted answered. But when he didn't, she realised with a rush of relief that the unbearable moment was over. Adam was worried about legalities. He wasn't going to announce any terrible news about himself and Sally. Not yet, anyhow.

Feeling just a little calmer, she moved to the drawer where the cutlery was stored and began to select knives and forks. 'So how much success have you had with your inquiries?' she made herself ask. 'Have you been able to find Sally?'

'No luck at all so far,' he admitted with a loud sigh. 'I can't get a clue out of anyone. I've tried the paper where she worked, but they said she's quit and hasn't left a forwarding address. I've tried your family. None of them seems to have a flaming clue. It's like she's vanished into thin air.'

'We'll just have to be patient,' Claire surprised herself by saying. 'Sally said in her letter she wanted to give us time to adjust.'

Adam shrugged his reluctant agreement and flipped the microwave door open.

An attitude of patience and calm was what Claire desperately longed for, but over the following week she discovered that it wasn't something she could simply switch on.

Not when Adam seemed preoccupied and eager to take off to the far ends of Nardoo each morning. Not when poor little Rosco continued to be unsettled and most especially not when there was so much to think about.

While she completed the final preparations for Adam's birthday party, she also had to divide her days between caring for the baby and trying not to think about his parentage. After years of desperately longing for a baby, she didn't dare complain to anyone that coping with Rosco was difficult.

What would they think of her? She'd find herself nominated as the Ungrateful Woman of the Year.

And after planning the party for so many months, she couldn't back out of it now. Adam's friends from far and wide were looking forward to next Saturday night's celebration.

There was still so much to do. A suitable garden table had to be found to serve drinks from. She still hadn't decided on the best way to light the garden paths that led from the front of the house around to the party area in the new courtyard.

Final decisions had to be made about floral decorations and Claire elected to use Adam's favourite deep red roses from the garden. There were masses of them in bloom at the moment and she could arrange them informally in bowls and silver beakers. Fallen rose petals could be scattered on the serving tables for a romantic touch.

Nancy and Claire had already made special napkin rings from gold tassels and cord. Now, while Rosco slept in his little capsule on the floor beside them, they washed the best fine white and gold china and set it aside in a spare room ready for use. The silver needed polishing and the gilt-tinged crystal glasses had to be rubbed with soft cloths until they were sparkling.

Nancy's husband Joe drove into Daybreak and bought all the last-minute perishable items for the party and he collected Adam's dinner suit which Claire had sent to the dry-cleaners so it could be ready for the event.

The wines, beer and soft drink were stowed away in the cold room. Claire and Nancy kept a close eye on the weather forecasts and they made lists of all their last-minute cooking tasks and allocated a time schedule for each job.

They elected to keep the canapés simple. Blinis with

smoked salmon curls and oriental style rice-paper wraps with spicy soy dipping sauce. The heart-shaped birthday cake was already baked and was being decorated by one of Nancy's nieces and she would bring it in from Daybreak on the day.

But instead of going about the tasks of preparation in a flurry of excited anticipation, Claire had to work with the weight of a constant gnawing sadness. The question of Rosco's father loomed larger in her mind all the time.

She found that her days were exhausting but almost manageable.

The nights were more of a problem.

It was harder to push her dark doubts and worries aside at night. The nights brought Adam.

When he climbed into her bed, wearing nothing but boxer shorts, his long, strong body looking as gorgeous and sexy as ever, she wanted so much to reach out for him, to touch him and to feel the reassurance of his answering touch, of his arms enfolding her.

But she couldn't.

Not when she kept seeing him in her sister's bed.

When, for the third night in a row they went to bed and, once again, Claire avoided any physical contact, not even a hug and a kiss, Adam demanded answers. His patience was obviously worn to threads.

'What is it, Claire? You've got to tell me what's wrong.'

She gripped the sheet tightly to her. 'I think I'm going through some kind of nervous reaction,' she told him. 'I know I didn't give birth to Rosco, but I feel like I'm going through post-natal depression.'

It was hard to tell if Adam believed her, but he didn't push the issue at first. He just lay with his hands stacked under his head, staring at the ceiling and frowning, just as he had on that night last summer when they'd fought.

Finally, he gave a huge sigh and said he thought she'd sleep better if he was in another room. Claire's heart seemed to shrink in her chest, but she let him go without trying to stop him. She didn't want him to hear her crying.

Each night the tension grew worse.

She suspected she was behaving very badly. She knew she should confront Adam, get the whole problem out in the open, deal with it and work out where to go from there.

'I'll talk to him after the party,' she whispered to her white-faced reflection in the mirror. 'I couldn't go ahead with the party if I found out he'd been with Sally. And I've been planning it for so long...'

Once, when Rosco cried for his early-morning feed, she couldn't summon the strength to get out of bed. She lay there listening as the baby's cries crescendoed and felt very sorry for herself. It was ages before she finally forced her legs over the edge of the bed and stumbled out to the kitchen to fetch his bottle.

Adam was already there.

'I'll look after him,' he told her. 'Go back to bed. You need to sleep. You've been looking very tired.'

She should have thanked him, but was hit by an unexpected thought. Why should I thank him? It's *his* baby. Hardly believing she could be so ungrateful, she hurried back to bed without a word.

And so the week continued. The worst seven days of her life.

Claire knew the close-knit fabric of their marriage wasn't just fraying, it was unravelling at frightening speed. She didn't have to push Adam away any more.

He was already distant. It wasn't just their sex life that disappeared, but all the little things, too. The loving glances, the brief but tender touches, the sharing of news at the end of the day. All the tiny stitches that had been gathering and securing their lives together.

Over the years, these moments had supplied them with a thousand reassurances that they loved each other. As well as the sustained passionate edge that had always kept them alight and on fire for each other, there had been a deeper, stronger love.

It had begun gently in the early years of their marriage, the way dawn arrived in the bush lighting the treetops and the homestead roofs till it filtered through to strengthen and warm the whole land.

Like the sun, their love had become the source of light and energy that strengthened their lives. Now, in a matter of days, they'd reached the point where they were both so edgy, so cold, so exhausted, they could no longer reach each other.

Every night, life became more unbearable.

The storm broke when Adam came home on Friday evening to find Claire in the study weeping over a book as if her heart would break.

She slammed the book shut as soon as he entered the room, but when she looked at him she couldn't hide her face and she knew it was red and swollen from crying.

'I've had as much of this as I can take.' His voice was cold with anger as he walked stiffly towards her. 'I know there's something really upsetting you and I'm sick of having you fob me off with stories about hormones or depression. I'm sure that's not the problem. It's something to do with me, isn't it?'

Her heart thundered as he waited, stony-faced, for her answer. She wanted to shake her head, to deny it. This was the moment she'd been avoiding. Did she have to do this now? She'd been hoping to find more strength before the showdown.

'Time's up, Claire, you've got to tell me.'

'This isn't the night to talk about it,' she protested.

His arms rose slowly. Crossing them over his chest, he squared his wide shoulders and eyed her steadily. 'It's got to be tonight.'

'But it's your birthday tomorrow.'

'My birthday?' he almost shouted. 'Hip hip hooray! It won't be much of a celebration if you're getting around with a face longer than a wet week.' He unfolded his arms and stepped forward to touch her tear-stained cheek with surprising gentleness.

'Oh, Adam,' she sobbed. 'I'm sorry.'

He pulled his hand away and shoved it in his jeans pocket. 'So am I. We seem to have ourselves in a bloody mess.' Both hands safely in his pockets now, he stepped away and stared through a window to the river. He cast her a bleak glance over his shoulder. 'Maybe I could handle this better if I had even a tiny clue as to what your problem is.'

'I can't believe you don't know,' she whispered.

CHAPTER TEN

ADAM'S head was pounding as he turned away from the window and faced Claire. 'Believe me. I can't for the life of me work out why this has happened to us.'

This time he wouldn't give in until he had the truth out of her. No matter how painful her revelation was, he was damn sure it couldn't be any worse than what he'd been going through for this past gut-tearing week.

Every muscle in his body seemed to be clenched in an agony of tension; every nerve ending jarred as he waited for her response.

She unclasped the hands that had been tightly held in her lap and pushed herself out of the chair. Without looking at him, she said, 'You can't pretend you don't know who Rosco's father is.'

Rosco's father!

What the hell was she talking about?

'How could I possibly know anything about that?'

'Oh, Adam, for God's sake. Don't pretend. It's so obvious.'

Claire was twisting her hands together again, but her dark eyes smouldered with accusation.

His heart booming in his ears, Adam felt thoroughly alarmed, as if he'd been cornered in the stockyards by a wild-eyed steer. He recognised the familiar tension in his body as it prepared for conflict, but his mind simply wanted to escape from this nightmare. 'What are you saying?'

'I'm sure you don't need me to spell it out.'

'You think—you think *I'm* the father?' *Is that what this is all about?*

Her chin came up defiantly. 'Yes.'

The shock caught him as if he'd been punched by a drunken ringer. He'd never heard anything so insane. He felt sickened by waves of conflicting emotion…disbelief…anger…frustration. 'Claire, that's completely and utterly *crazy!*'

'You didn't think it was so crazy when you sat in the kitchen with Sally last summer having a nice little early-morning chat.'

He forced his mind back to her sister's visit. To his conversation with Sally. 'You're saying I went behind your back with Sally's crazy turkey-baster idea?'

Surely not. He searched Claire's face for a response, a denial, an assurance of her trust in him.

The only thing he saw was dark, unmistakable suspicion.

He took two steps towards her, both arms outstretched, ready to shove these stupid doubts out of her mind and into the next state.

But when he saw the way Claire almost jumped behind the chair, as if she needed a physical barrier between them, he stopped short, as if he'd run into one of his own electric fences.

It was then he understood. With a nauseating flood of disbelief, he realised what was *really* bugging Claire. His throat felt strangled as he made himself ask, 'You think I did more than that, don't you?'

In dismay he watched as Claire suddenly went limp. She gripped the back of a chair for support and turned her head away.

'Claire, tell me.'

His heart clattered wildly when he saw her nod.

This was beyond insane. 'I can't believe you think that.'

She made no response.

'You really believe I've been keeping something from you ever since Sally came up with her hare-brained scheme?'

Slowly, Claire's tear-blotched, wretched face turned his way. 'You've got to tell me, Adam. Did you supply Sally with—with what she needed for a clinical fertilisation?'

'Hell, no!'

Her eyes closed and he thought she was going to be sick.

'So you did…the *other*,' she whispered.

He couldn't believe the choking hurt in his throat, the weight of grief in his chest.

'You think we got together? Me and your little sister had it off behind your back?'

He checked his hands, sure that they were shaking with emotion, but they were gripped tightly by his sides. 'Is *that* what all this has been about?' he asked.

But Claire slumped back into the chair and, leaning forward onto the desk, buried her face in her hands.

Adam rushed closer. 'Don't go silent on me now, Claire. We've got to finish this.'

He almost grabbed her shoulders and wrenched her around, forcing her to face him. But he was afraid that if he touched her, he might hurt her. He'd never laid a hand on Claire in anger and he wasn't about to start now.

After an agonising stretch of time, she lifted her face to look at him.

'Adam, I don't know how you did it. I think I know *why* you did it…' the new calmness in her voice was a fresh shock '…but it's time for some honesty.' Her brown eyes were surprisingly steady as she added, 'You know how much I wanted this baby, but you should have told me what you were doing…both of you.'

'Maybe there was nothing to tell.'

'Everyone knows little Rosco is the spitting image of you.'

Everyone? Was it possible to detonate on the spot? This was going from bad to worse to absolute fiasco. 'What do you mean *everyone* knows? You talk like the whole bloody district is in on this…*everyone except me*!' He knew he was shouting now, but this latest news was beyond the pale. He couldn't help letting fly.

'Nancy and Joe have seen the resemblance. Adam, anyone who looks at little Rosco can see you staring back at them… It's only…it's only to be expected.'

'Oh, that's great.' Adam laughed bitterly. 'Oh, that's rich, Claire. The whole district would *expect* your sister's kid to look like me.'

She ignored his logic. 'It's the secrecy that has hurt me most. I thought we were so close, Adam. I never imagined there'd be any secrets in our marriage.'

With a curse, he paced away from her, across the room. *How crazy can life get?* Without even asking him, Claire had taken it upon herself to assume he'd had sex with Sally.

He clamped spread palms to his temple as he shook his head… If he'd ever had any fantasies about his kid sister-in-law, they had never surfaced. But Claire's imagination must have been working overtime. She'd been picturing Sally in bed with him. She'd convinced herself it had really happened. Sally surrendering her body so Claire could have a baby. *His* baby.

He moaned and slid his palms lower, pressing them into his eyes.

No! This can't be happening to us.

He felt drained, more exhausted than he'd ever known. A week's mustering in rough country, long hours sleeping in the saddle, nothing could compare to the emotional exhaustion that engulfed him now.

'Claire, Rosco is not mine. There's no way Sally and I—'

'Don't say any more. It's so unlike you to—'

'To lie to you? You know I've never lied to you, Claire, and yet you don't believe me.'

For a moment, he thought he'd made a connection. She frowned and her dark chocolate eyes were shadowed with uncertainty, but then her mouth pursed and she shook her head. 'I want to believe you. Until now there has never been any reason to doubt you, but how do you explain the amazing resemblance...the family resemblance?'

Her fingers shook as they traced the edges of the book in front of her on the desk. 'Whenever I look at Rosco, I can't help but see you at the same time... It's eating me up, Adam. I mean, the only rational explanation is that you and Sally went ahead with her suggestion.'

'You call that rational?' Adam couldn't hold back a four-letter expletive. 'If the poor little bloke really does look like me, it's just a coincidence, a million-to-one, or a zillion-to-one chance. I don't know how your sister did it but she didn't do it with...'

With an angry snap of her wrist, Clare flipped open the book she'd been fiddling with. It was a photo album. Adam hadn't seen it in years, but now he recognised it as his parents' album. Quickly she flicked past pages of wedding photos until she reached a collection of snaps of a mother and a baby.

Fine hairs rose on the back of his neck. He took a step closer and then another.

He stared at the baby lying in his mother's arms. Rosco's little face peered back at him and his mouth turned dry as dust.

Dimly, he was aware of Claire looking his way. Her eyes were tallying a clinical assessment of his features, from his dark hair to the cleft in his chin—like a computer system trying to match up forensic evidence. There was no warmth or emotion in her gaze.

'Would you like me to turn side on for another angle?' he asked coldly.

She flushed red, then shrugged her shoulders. 'What are you going to do about it?'

'What am *I* going to do?' he shouted, incredulous. 'What *can* I do? I'm amazed you haven't run the poor little fellow into Daybreak and had him swabbed for a DNA test.'

Claire shouted back just as loudly. 'You take it up with Rosco's mother first. Have a long heart-to-heart talk with that little sister of mine... That shouldn't be so hard considering what great pals you are.'

Stunned, Adam stared at the woman he loved. The woman who meant more to him than life itself.

He'd always considered that meeting Claire Tremaine was the best thing that had ever happened to him. The very best thing.

'Do you realise what you're saying?' he asked. 'You don't trust me.'

She closed her eyes and sat very still, her mouth pulled in tight and pale.

Claire had always been The One. The Grand Passion in his life. But this hard, embittered creature was not the woman he'd married. This woman who shrank from his touch as if she detested him was someone else completely. How little she must have thought of him that she believed he could cheat on her like that.

Where had *his* Claire gone? How the *hell* had he lost her?

Facing disaster, Adam did what he'd always done. He considered his options and made a decision. There was really only one path he could take.

It was an unthinkable, unbearable solution, but Claire left him no choice.

'If you insist,' he said and he felt sick to the stomach, as if he were facing death, as if he were speaking to her for the very last time, 'I'll go find your sister. But don't expect me back for a while.'

Spinning on his heel, he marched straight out of the room.

'Adam, wait a moment. Come back!'

Claire jumped to her feet, but her legs shook so badly she could hardly stand.

He kept walking briskly away from her.

'Adam!'

There was absolutely no sign that he heard.

Horrified, Claire stumbled after him as he marched, stiff-backed, through the lounge and down the hall to their bedroom. He was going to leave her. Oh, God, no! This couldn't be happening. She needed to know the truth about Rosco, but she didn't want it at this price. She'd never wanted Adam to leave.

Heart in mouth, she followed him, her head swimming with a thousand desperate thoughts.

Why was he reacting so fiercely? She had never seen Adam look so angry, hadn't known he was capable of such anger.

Had he been hurt by her accusations? Was it because he was guilty?

Would he come back?

When?

She clamped a shaking hand to her mouth. Heavens, what on earth would she do about the party?

He was striding quickly into the bedroom and, from the doorway, she watched as he wrenched the top drawer of his dresser open. With rough movements, he snatched up a duffle bag and swept the contents of the drawer into it. Then he opened his wardrobe, ripped some shirts from their hangers and tossed them in, too.

Claire sagged against the door frame, watching him in horror. 'Adam, don't do this. What can you achieve by going?'

'I've told you exactly what I'm hoping to achieve.' Hefting the duffle bag onto one shoulder, he sidestepped around her, back through the doorway.

'But you can't go now!' she cried after his retreating back.

He continued on down the hall to the front door. 'Just watch me.'

She couldn't let him go like this. She would have to tell him about the party. If Adam knew there were so many people coming for his birthday...

His truck was parked in the front drive and he jumped down the three front steps and threw the bag into its tray back.

'Adam!' Claire cried. 'What about tomorrow? It's your birthday.'

Ignoring her, he pulled the driver's door open and swung his long body into the front seat. He held the door open as he looked back at her for a brief, wretched moment. Then he slammed the truck's door shut and the engine whirred to life.

Claire couldn't believe he was going just like that.

No goodbye…

She couldn't bear to stand there and watch him drive away. With a broken sob, she spun around and staggered back into the house, so blinded by tears that she banged her hip hard against the door frame. Behind her, she heard tyres spin on the gravel as Adam took off.

And from inside the house came the sound of Rosco crying.

She stood stock-still in the middle of the hallway and wanted to die. Adam had left her. In a handful of heartbeats, her beautiful, wonderful man was gone. Instead she had a baby.

How ludicrous was that? All these years she'd wanted a baby and now she had one. *But at what dreadful price?*

Her legs threatened to give way completely now and she was forced to lean against the wall. How had it happened that she had a baby instead of Adam?

She'd gained a baby and lost a husband.

Lost a husband!

The terrible truth was so suddenly, blindingly obvious, she moaned aloud. A deep, agonising sound. How could she have been so foolish as to have missed it till now?

Adam meant more to her than any baby.

All those years she'd felt empty without a baby were nothing compared with the ghastly, deathlike hollowness that opened inside her now.

She loved her husband! Why, without Adam, there was no point in living. No point at all.

She didn't care what he'd done. She couldn't go on without him.

That shocking realisation sent her sliding down the wall until she ended in a crumpled heap on the hall floor.

CHAPTER ELEVEN

'ADAM! What are you doing here?'

Stretched out on his brother's shabby sofa, Adam looked up to discover Jack filling the doorway and looking predictably surprised to see him.

'I'm enjoying the comfort of your delightful lounge room.' He pointed with a remote control towards the television set. 'And watching a fascinating wildlife show about sea eagles in Far Eastern Russia.'

Jack gave a disbelieving roll of his eyes as he ambled into the room. It was a typical living room in a bachelor pad—minimal second-hand furniture, paperbacks, magazines and old newspapers stacked on the floor for want of bookshelves, the odd dirty coffee-cup and beer bottle lying around.

'How did you get in?' he asked.

'Ah.' Adam depressed a button on the remote to switch off the set. ' I must confess that I broke in. Did you know you have a window almost off its hinges conveniently close to the back door?' He jumped to his feet and extended his hand to Jack. 'Good to see you, little brother.'

Jack returned the handshake, but as he eyed Adam his expression remained distinctly puzzled. 'How long have you been here?'

'Actually, I arrived last night, but obviously you weren't at home.' With what he hoped was a placating smile, Adam settled back onto the sofa.

But Jack Townsend remained standing. A little shorter and burlier than his older brother, he stood with his feet wide apart in the middle of the room, one thumb spinning his keyring round and round his index finger. His dark brows and blue eyes, not quite such a deep hue as Adam's, were fixed in a sharp frown.

'Been busy?' Adam asked, wishing Jack wouldn't make it so darn obvious that this sudden visit was completely out of character. 'I figured when you weren't here that you must have had a big job on one of the outlying properties and needed to stay away overnight.'

'Yeah, I've been busier than a one-armed milker on a dairy farm. Been away for just over a week, actually. Not enough vets out this way.' Jack continued to frown at Adam, then he tossed the keys into an empty ashtray on top of his television before he asked, 'But why didn't you tell me you were coming into town last night? What's going on?'

For the past twenty-four hours, Adam had been trying to come up with the best way to answer this question. He knew it was inevitable and completely justified that Jack would demand an explanation. He was hoping Jack might hold the solution to all his problems.

It was too painful to go into details about leaving Claire, but there was no use in beating about the bush. 'I was hoping you could help me.'

For the first time, Jack grinned. 'Wow. I'm flattered.' Cocking his head to one side, he pulled an exaggerated grimace as if he was pretending to think hard. 'I don't remember my big brother ever needing my help before. Correction—ever *asking* for my help before.'

Adam managed to crack a grin. 'You know what they say about a first time for everything.'

Jack headed for a lounge chair. He was about to take a seat when he looked at his watch then swung around, staring at Adam strangely. 'Hang on a sec,' he said. 'You shouldn't be here, mate. It's six o'clock. 'Struth! I haven't got time to sit here gas-bagging with you, either.'

'Sorry,' said Adam quickly. 'If you have somewhere to go, don't let me hold you up.'

'If I've got somewhere to go?' Jack repeated. '*You're* the one with somewhere to go. You're the guest of honour!'

'What are you talking about?'

Jack's mouth opened and his light blue eyes rounded. He stood gaping at Adam. His mouth remained hanging open for five full seconds before he snapped it shut again. 'Hell. I forgot it's a surprise. You don't know.'

'What don't I know?'

Jack sank into the chair and, with an elbow propped on its arm, rubbed his temple while he stared at the fuzzy yellow rays of the setting sun as they slanted through a window and lit up the dust on his timber floorboards.

'Jack,' Adam said. 'I've had a pretty rough time of it in the past twenty-four hours. Don't mess me about. What's going on?'

'Er...' Jack hesitated. 'You said you wanted some help. You'd better tell me what's the matter, mate. I've seen dropped meat pies that look in better shape than you do right now.'

'Are you sure you've got time to talk? What's this thing you have to go to?'

'I'll explain in a minute. First things first. You fill me in about your problem.'

Letting his hips slide forward, Adam settled a little lower on the sofa with his arms spread along its back and his legs stretched out in front of him. He wanted to look as relaxed as possible. No mean feat when he'd been in a complete tail-spin all day. 'It's not a problem exactly. But I need to track down Sally.'

'Sally?' Jack suddenly sat very straight, as if he'd been switched onto high alert.

The reaction didn't surprise Adam. In fact it gave him hope. 'You know who I mean. Claire's sister. Sally Tremaine, the journalist.'

'Yeah,' Jack said, swallowing. ' Of course, I know her. We were best man and bridesmaid at your wedding. But why do you want to find her?'

'Well…you know this baby of hers…'

'This *what*?' Jack's face paled visibly and his knuckles whitened as he clutched the arms of his lounge chair.

'The baby. A little boy—Rosco.'

'Sally's had a baby?' Jack's voice was almost a whisper.

With mounting dismay, Adam watched his brother's shocked face. Maybe he was barking up the wrong tree. He'd been putting two and two together. Sally had seen Jack last summer. He'd been so relieved when it had struck him that Rosco could well be his brother's son.

'He was born nearly a month ago.'

'Dead set? A month ago? Where?'

'I don't know where he was born, but he's at our place now—at Nardoo. Sally more or less dumped him on our doorstep.'

Jack looked as if he was having trouble breathing.

'You OK, mate?' Adam asked.

He watched as his brother ploughed tense fingers into his thick dark hair. 'I—I'm fine,' Jack said. After a while, he seemed to give himself a mental shake-down. 'So Sally's palmed her kid off onto Claire, has she?'

'Claire's looking after him,' Adam admitted. 'But, actually, Sally's *given* him to Claire—to us. It's all Sally's idea. Some crazy idea of a gift—because we haven't been able to have a baby of our own.'

Jack managed a weak smile. 'I can imagine Sally coming up with a wacky scheme like that.'

'Yeah. Problem is she's disappeared and, well—we need to get a few things sorted out. It's all a bit—messy.'

Jack jumped to his feet and began to pace the floor. 'Let me get this straight. Sally's had a baby and she's handed it over to you and then taken off. And now you're looking for her.'

'That's it.'

'OK. I've got that, but what I don't understand is why you're looking for her now? Why tonight? Couldn't it have waited till tomorrow? What's Claire think about you running out on your birthday party?'

Adam shrugged. 'I have a birthday every year. Finding Sally is more important.'

'But you don't have a huge slap-up party with half the district invited every year.'

'Of course not,' Adam responded snappily. Then Jack's words sank in. 'Half the district? What are you saying?'

'You mutton head. Claire's been planning a party for months. You're supposed to be at Nardoo now, dressed up to the nines and welcoming the first of your guests.'

A party? The thought made Adam dizzy. He remembered last night. Claire running after him, calling out that it was his birthday. 'Don't worry,' he said dully. 'Claire will have cancelled it.'

Jack gave a snort of disbelief. 'Believe me, big brother. She won't have cancelled this party. It's been too big a deal for her. She's rung me several times to help with the ordering and, I could tell by the tone of her voice, she's been as excited as a pig in muck for weeks.'

'Well, she won't be excited any more. I walked out on

her last night.' The words seemed to echo in Adam's head and trample on his heart as he said them.

'Walked out?'

Jack lowered himself onto the arm of the sofa and leaned close to take a long, hard look at his brother. 'Jesus,' he whispered. 'You don't mean you walked out—as in *left* her?'

Had he? Was that really what he'd done?

He'd jumped into the truck and scorched off the property, too hurt and too damn angry over her crazy accusation to sort out emotion from reason.

It hadn't really occurred to him that he'd been racing away from his marriage, but he'd been too full of steam to think clearly.

Twenty-four hours later, he still couldn't make sense of what had happened. He certainly couldn't come near explaining to Jack what it had felt like when Claire had thrown her mistrust in his face—as if all those years of fidelity suddenly meant nothing.

He grimaced. 'I'd say Claire might be under the impression that I've left her. I told her not to expect me back for some time.'

He couldn't meet Jack's eyes, but in his peripheral vision he saw the way his brother tossed his head back and he heard his shocked, almost scared laugh.

'Pull the other one, Adam. You couldn't leave Claire. Blind Freddie could see that you and that woman are made for each other. And she's absolutely nuts about you, mate. You two have the kind of relationship they write songs about.'

Adam closed his eyes. He didn't need his little brother to tell him what he could be losing by walking out on Claire. He'd had a night and a day to think about it.

It would be like losing his own identity. Several times

he'd almost jumped in the truck and gone back. He wanted to charge into that house and explain in no uncertain terms just how badly she'd flipped about this.

But, hell! If she couldn't trust him, she wouldn't believe anything he said.

So he'd stayed here sweating, waiting for Jack in the vain hope his brother could help him find Sally. Even if he wasn't the father, she'd visited him last summer. Perhaps he had a clue. On this matter, he had no one else to turn to.

But it had been a hell of a day. Beating off memories was the worst. He kept remembering so much... Too much...

Right back to the day more than nine years ago when he and Claire had met. It had been on one of his trips to Melbourne when he'd taken his mother for her annual shopping spree.

While Elizabeth Townsend had haunted exclusive boutiques in Toorak, Adam had walked the inner city streets, visiting art galleries, the museum and the bookshops.

It had been in a bookshop in Collins Street that he and Claire had backed into each other. Literally. They'd both been so absorbed in their reading that other shoppers had been forced to move around them, the way flowing water moved around boulders in a stream.

He'd been thumbing through a book about the American Civil War and Claire had been looking at a huge coffee-table book about cottage gardens. At the same moment, they both must have realised they were blocking people's way so they stepped back.

And had collided.

Full of apologies, they'd turned to face each other.

And that was all it had taken.

There had been a startling, unmistakable moment of

instant awareness. Adam had found himself immobilised by dark, chocolate eyes. Claire had stared straight back at him and smiled. Oh, boy! What a smile that had been! It had clinched a moment of connection.

They'd hardly cared where they'd dumped the books back on the shelves. Adam could never remember exactly what he'd said when he'd invited her to the café next door for coffee, but Claire had accepted. And by the time they'd walked out of the bookshop they'd both known they had fallen hopelessly in love at first sight.

Jack's noisy swearing brought Adam back to the present with a lurch of raw pain.

'I told Claire not to expect me back till I find Sally and get everything sorted out,' Adam told him. 'So, if she was planning a party for tonight, I'd say she'll go ahead and have it without me.'

Jack let out his breath on a long, ragged sigh. 'I can't imagine what's going on in your crazy head, man.'

Adam's jaw hardened. 'It's not half as crazy as what's going on in Claire's. Now, tell me, can you help me find Sally?'

CHAPTER TWELVE

BENEATH a slender new moon, the new courtyard at Nardoo homestead rippled with conversation. Fifty guests were seated under a white timber pergola that had been transformed into a fragrant fairyland of climbing roses and strings of tiny lights.

They were dining at long trestle tables covered with snowy white Italian linen. In the middle of the tables stood candles in glass holders and silver urns spilling with plush roses, deep red, as rich as burgundy velvet.

The glassware gleamed as guests sipped wine. Laughter tinkled. From the river below, a pleasant zephyr breeze drifted. Everyone was enjoying their marinated roast lamb or braised veal shank served with polenta triangles and salsa verde.

Everyone except the woman sitting at the head of one table.

Claire looked exquisite in the outfit she'd ordered from an exclusive Melbourne store. The halter-necked organza creation was the colour of the palest, most expensive champagne. Its neck and waist were richly embroidered with gold beading and the bodice and skirt were dotted all over with tiny gold sequins.

When she'd seen her reflection in the mirror earlier in the evening, she had been stunned by how well it suited her. It had looked so good she'd almost ripped it off and pulled out something else. Anything would do. She'd bought *this* outfit for Adam.

For weeks she'd been looking forward to seeing his

139

eyes when she first appeared in it. She knew she'd never worn anything before that showed off her good points quite so well. Somehow its subtle, delicate colour blended with her complexion, her eyes and her hair to flatter her beyond expectation.

Her guests had all remarked on how lovely she looked and what a dreadful pity it was that Adam had been called away at the last minute.

Of course, it had been too late to call off the party. By the time she'd gathered her wits and wondered if she should cancel, she'd realised that, to travel the long distance to reach them in time, some folk would have left home already.

Nancy had insisted that the party must go on. She'd been dreadfully upset when Claire had told her that she and Adam had quarrelled and that he'd gone away, but once she'd recovered she'd urged Claire to tell her guests a white lie.

'You can make up a story about one of those uncles of Adam's. You know—his mother had a couple of bachelor brothers up in Cape York. One of them could have died suddenly and Adam had to go away to the funeral.'

'Oh, Nancy, I'm already in a mess. I can't tell a lie as well. It could get out of hand. Just imagine if one of his uncles heard.'

In the end, she told her guests that her idea for a surprise party had flopped. Adam had had to leave on urgent business and, by the time he'd learned that he would miss his own party, it had been too late to change his plans. It was almost the truth.

People had been very understanding.

'Such a pity.'

'Poor Adam. What difficult timing. And when you have the new baby to care for.'

'Bad call. But not much you could do about it, lass.'

She quickly directed the conversation to happier topics.
'What a good season we've had this year.'

'Have you seen the courtyard? I'm so pleased with the
way it's turned out.'

But now the opening pleasantries were over. The
guests had met and mingled and mellowed with the help
of champagne. Curious women had been satisfied by a
peek at the baby, asleep in his cot, bless him. They'd
been politely lacking in curiosity about his parentage and
had wished her well with the adoption process.

Then they had all settled in to enjoy the meal and the
evening.

And Claire was left with her misery.

She couldn't enjoy any of it. The food seemed dry and
tasteless and the wine bitter. The beautiful canopy of stars
above them lit the lazy river so that it glowed with a
pearly radiance, but the very beauty of the evening
seemed to mock her.

*What kind of fool are you, Claire? You go to all this
trouble. Your garden, your clothes... You are surrounded
by beauty—the countryside, this perfect night... But what
does it matter? You've thrown away the only thing that
mattered. You've thrown away Adam. Fool... you silly little fool.*

She wanted wings. To fly away. To leave her guests.
To abandon Nancy and her nieces working stalwartly in
the kitchen.

One of her closest friends from a neighbouring station
leaned closer and her eyes rested for a moment on the
untouched food on Claire's plate. 'Claire, is something
wrong?'

'No!' she answered just a little too brightly. 'Ah...I
wonder if we'll have an early wet season this

year? Have you heard what the long-range forecasters are saying?'

Oh, man! She knew her friend wouldn't let her get away with such a pathetic response, but before she had time to be embarrassed they were distracted suddenly by an excited shout from the far end of the courtyard.

Heads turned and Claire looked up.

'Look who's arrived,' a voice cried.

The path leading from the front of the house was lit by the rows of thick pillar candles that Claire had placed in white paper cylinders and anchored with river sand.

Along the path came two figures. Two masculine figures. The light from the candles didn't reach their faces, but Claire could see dark trousers and the deep, V-shaped gleam of white shirt fronts beneath elegant black jackets.

There were excited calls of greeting. People were jumping to their feet. Claire's magnified heartbeats and breathing were so loud she couldn't hear what anyone was saying but soon she saw who was there.

First came Jack…

And then…Adam.

Despite the difference in their height, they looked ridiculously alike in their matching dinner suits.

All around her were cries of 'Happy Birthday!' and 'Adam, how wonderful that you could make it after all!'

Claire swayed in her seat as she heard his deep voice apologising for being late.

Why had he come? Had he found Sally? Her stomach was so tightly clenched she was glad she hadn't eaten. It would hardly do if she threw up all over the guest of honour.

After what seemed like ages, Adam looked her way. She was still in her chair and, for the life of her, she couldn't be sure that she wasn't superglued to the spot.

She had no idea if her legs would work if she tried to stand.

Down the length of the table, their gazes met. And suddenly the voices of the guests stilled.

Claire gulped. She knew everybody would be expecting her to greet her husband. They all knew that this was a wonderful, happy, out-of-the-blue surprise. The answer to her prayers.

Adam wasn't smiling at her. She suspected he was no more capable of smiling than she was. The evening crackled with the hushed, expectant silence of the assembled guests.

Don't make a scene! a voice in Claire's head warned. *Be calm and act natural. You're allowed to be surprised. Adam was called away...you weren't expecting him.*

'Adam.' The word came out as a whisper and she doubted that anybody heard it. Clearing her throat, she tried again. 'Hi, Adam.' This time her voice sounded almost normal. She placed her hands on the table in front of her and pushed herself to her feet.

Her legs felt as wobbly as blancmange but they held.

He was staring at her. His throat was working as his eyes took in her elegant dress, her bare shoulders and arms.

And she was staring back at him. Heaven help her. He had never tugged at her heart as he did now with his brittle smile carefully in place. Somehow he looked darker, harder, almost a stranger.

Claire wanted to run to him, to wrap her arms around him and kiss away that hurt, hard pride in his eyes, to welcome him back and beg his forgiveness and who cared what the onlookers thought? She took a faltering step and swayed against the table. Oh, dear. Had anybody seen how she was trembling?

If only they would stop looking…

Then at last he came down the length of the table towards her.

'I couldn't miss this splendid party,' he said, placing two hands on her shoulders and leaning forward. Heart fluttering, she raised her face to his. He kissed her briefly on the cheek, then withdrew his hands quickly and stepped away.

Polite, brotherly, it was over in an instant. The kind of kiss Jack might have given her.

Claire tried not to let her disappointment show.

She couldn't think of what to say and asked the first thing that came into her head. 'Where did you get the dinner suit?'

'It belongs to a friend of Jack's.' He wriggled his shoulders a little, as if the jacket was too tight.

A jocular male voice called loudly, 'Claire scrubs up all right when she puts the warpaint on, doesn't she, mate?'

Adam cast her a scorching, tight-lipped glance. 'Absolutely,' he said softly.

But although she smarted from Adam's coolness, Claire could have kissed the man who had spoken. His rough words broke the ice. Soon everyone was chatting again. Glasses were being refilled.

Cutlery, plates and wineglasses were brought out and Jack's and Adam's places were set. Adam sat some distance away from Claire. The men were plied with food and drink.

The party continued.

Adam was sure his face would crack if he had to hold his smile much longer. It helped if he didn't look Claire's way. To look and to know that he couldn't touch was torture.

He ached when he saw how very beautiful she looked tonight. Her new gown enhanced her delicate air, making her look like the beautifully fragile glass angel she'd brought back from Venice last summer. A glass angel whose dark eyes were shadowed by unmistakable pain.

One glance her way and his heart felt as if it, too, were made of glass and on the verge of shattering.

Starlight painted her skin with a mysterious pale sheen and turned her soft golden hair to shimmering silver. She looked ethereal. An unattainable mirage.

Or was that impression exaggerated by the unreality of this hoax?

It was ridiculous to be making a public spectacle of himself, pretending that everything was fine and dandy. Coming back like this was the last thing he'd wanted, but Jack had given him little choice when they'd thrashed the issue out earlier in the evening.

'You're going to this party if I have to put a headlock on you or tie you up and throw you in the back of the ute,' Jack shouted.

These days, bluffing Jack wasn't as easy as it had been when he was ten years old, but Adam tried. 'You haven't got a hope, little brother. I'm not going back to Nardoo till I find Sally Tremaine.'

Jack's face tightened. 'What information exactly do you need to get from Sally?'

'I need to know who her baby's father is.'

For a full ten seconds his brother looked as if he was fighting for his breath. 'You don't have any idea who the father is?' he managed to ask at last.

'That's the whole flaming problem. Claire's decided the kid looks the spitting image of me and...' Adam's eyes narrowed. 'People have commented before today on how alike we look. I thought that perhaps you could help me find the truth.'

Ploughing agitated hands through his hair, Jack paced the room. 'I swear I don't know anything about Sally's baby,' he said at last. 'But if you're any sort of man you'll go back to this party tonight and do the right thing by your wife and your bloody self and—' A dark sigh escaped. 'And I guess I'd better tell you how you can contact Sally.'

Adam leapt from his seat. 'You know where she is?'

Jack's smile was tinged with bitterness. 'Yeah. I've got a contact number.'

'How come you didn't tell me before? I've got to speak to her right away. I don't want to waste time on this.'

'I won't tell you a thing if you don't come to the party.'

'Jack, damn it, this is blackmail.'

'It's the deal, Adam. Tomorrow morning I'll tell you where you can find Sally on the condition that you come back to Nardoo tonight.'

'Tomorrow morning? Why wait till then? I want to clear this up now.'

With an impatient sigh, Jack tapped the watch on his wrist. 'Because we don't have time now, thickhead. We should have left for the party fifteen minutes ago and we still have to find you a dinner suit.'

And here he was…at his own birthday party, surrounded by his oldest and dearest friends and feeling as lonely as a bandicoot on a burnt ridge.

God help him. In the past week, he and Claire had become strangers.

What could he achieve by seeing her again when he

still had no answers? If only he could have been confronting Sally right now. She was the key to this whole miserable debacle and the quicker he got to her, the better.

But he couldn't become too self-absorbed. He owed it to his guests to play the game. These were people he'd known all his life, with friendship bonds reaching back to childhood and even beyond that to earlier generations. He didn't want to snap their ties with one bad mood.

Had they noticed he was below par? Was that why they were even more exuberant than usual? All around him, people were swapping yarns loudly, asking and answering questions, exchanging hilarious jokes. There was laughter. Loads of laughter.

Of course, Jack had been right to insist that he come. It was an important face-saving exercise to preserve Nardoo's good name. Over generations, his family had established a widespread reputation for good hospitality and long-lasting friendships.

Tonight was a duty. No matter how painful, it was a job that had to be done.

Memories of birthday parties in his childhood brought a wistful smile to his lips. Some of these guests had been guests way back then. When they'd been very young they'd played tame indoor games like pass the parcel, supervised by his mother, or there had been treasure hunts in the garden. Later things had been much more exciting with campdrafting competitions and camp-outs down on the river bank.

Even when he'd been away at boarding-school, birthdays had meant the arrival of a huge box of food from his mother—a rich fruit cake smelling sinfully of rum, home-made fudge, toffee and ginger biscuits—enough to put on a party for his entire dorm.

You had it too easy as a kid, mate, he told himself now. *Welcome to the real world, where a birthday party can be the worst night of your life.*

Eventually, when the meal was finished and Adam had endured the cutting of the birthday cake and the accompanying fuss, the night grew a little chilly and dew began to fall silently. Claire opened out the French doors between the lounge and dining rooms, as well as the doors opening onto the veranda, and people drifted inside to settle on comfortable sofas and fat floor cushions while they listened to music and drank coffee and port. Some danced.

As Adam mixed and mingled with the guests, he couldn't help noticing how well Claire carried out her role as hostess. How did she do it? He was such a mess, he could hardly concentrate to engage in sensible conversation, but she was gracious, elegant, poised, considerate. She worked the room skilfully, while carefully skirting around any groups talking with him.

At eleven o'clock, he sought out Jack. 'I've done my part of the bargain. Let's go.'

'Go? Already? The night's just a pup.'

With an impatient growl, Adam grabbed the lapel of Jack's suit coat. 'It's plenty late enough and I want to get out of here.'

Jack shook himself free. 'For pity's sake, cool it, mate. This is your thirty-fifth birthday in your own home. There's no curfew.'

'There is as far as I'm concerned.'

'You're not bloody Cinderella.' Jack shoved a tawny port into Adam's hand. 'I don't see any glass slippers on your feet and I'm pretty certain my ute's not going to turn into a pumpkin even if we stay here all night.'

With thin-lipped, deliberate precision, Adam replaced

the glass on a coaster on a nearby table. 'Staying on is not part of my plan. It never was. You know that, Jack. A deal's a deal and I've kept my part of the bargain. These people know I'm busy. Now I want to get back to your place and make that call to wherever Sally is.'

'You can't go until you've had a talk to Claire.'

Adam lowered his gaze. Just hearing Claire's name hurt! He stared at the floor and noticed someone had dropped a stuffed olive. It had been walked into the carpet. 'There's not a lot I can say to Claire at the moment,' he muttered.

All night he'd been trying to avoid speaking with her again. He couldn't bear to see the pain in her eyes whenever she looked at him. Another sad glimpse of her dark eyes would feel like a stab wound in his chest. If only he could pack ice around his heart! He wanted to make it numb.

'I've said all I need to say apart from thanking Claire for the party and wishing her goodnight.'

Jack shook his head. 'I don't understand any of this.'

Who does? Adam thought. 'But you'll come back with me now?'

He sighed. 'If you insist, but it's too late to ring Sally tonight.'

'That doesn't matter. I want out of here.' Adam turned away immediately, not giving himself any time for second thoughts before he made his way across the room towards Claire. She was talking to the Jensens, a middle-aged couple who ran the stock and station agency in Daybreak, and so he was obliged to chat with them for a minute or two.

When there was a lull in the conversation, he said quickly, 'Excuse me, Claire, but I need to push off now.'

If it was possible, her face grew even paler than it had been all evening. 'You're going?' she whispered.

There was an uncomfortable silence—one of those awkward moments where a few seconds could feel like hours. The Jensens smiled uncertainly and shuffled their feet, as if they wondered if they should make themselves scarce.

Claire looked as if she was about to cave in—as if her limbs were made of soft modelling clay. Her eyes were too bright and her lips trembled.

And more memories forced themselves on Adam. Memories of Claire's soft, sexy lips parting beneath his. Of his tongue delving her moist sweetness.

How many times had he kissed her? It would have to be thousands. Tens of thousands. Their mouths were best friends. Claire's kisses were so inviting, so…intimate, so intoxicating.

And as for the rest…

He felt a painful glob in his throat, an unaccustomed stinging behind his eyes and he was forced to blink.

What about all the many, many times he and Claire had made love? Their sex life was so intense. At times, they had shared pure lust, wild and playful and so fierce he'd feared he might hurt her.

At other times their lovemaking had been profoundly, beautifully intimate. Their bodies had come together and merged so completely, their very souls had embraced.

They were truly one.

And they'd never stopped needing each other. Not even now.

How had they ever got to this impasse?

But, of course, the answer was dead easy. Claire had taken a good long look at that baby…

Adam cleared his throat. It felt painfully raw, as if

someone had shoved a fistful of dry straw down his gullet. 'I'm sorry if I've had to mess up your party plans,' he said gruffly. 'But as you know—things—things came up that made it unavoidable.'

'Yes,' she managed to whisper. Her head jerked nervously in the direction of the kitchen as she asked, 'There—there's nothing you wish to discuss?'

Completely embarrassed now, the Jensens mumbled something about needing coffee and melted away.

'There's nothing to discuss at this stage,' Adam told her. 'I'll let you know as soon as the matter is finalised.'

'Adam.'

The hurt in her eyes forced him to look away. 'Yes?'

'I—I need to talk to you.'

'About?'

'About us.'

He knew he couldn't do it. Without the answers she needed, there could be no way forward. 'Not tonight, Claire.' Stooping, he touched his lips to her cold cheek. 'You've done a great job. It's been an excellent party.'

Then he hurried over to the Jensens, who'd retreated to a corner. As he shook their hands, he tried not to notice how puzzled and concerned they looked. Tried not to notice the effort Claire was making to hold herself together.

Quickly he circled the room, making hasty farewells. Then he nodded to Jack and together they walked out.

Breathe. Remember to breathe.

Claire turned away from the heart-shattering sight of Adam disappearing once more into the night. This time it felt even worse than it had the night before.

If I keep breathing, I can't die.

It would have been better if he hadn't come to the

party at all. Seeing him walk away for the second time was more than she could possibly bear.

If only he had taken a moment or two to speak with her in private, she would have told him how sorry she was and begged him to come back.

It only feels as if I'm dying. My heart only feels as if it's about to erupt. All I have to do is keep breathing and I'll get through this.

This evening, she hadn't been able to keep her eyes off Adam and yet she'd found it unbearably painful to watch him. He was so cold and hard. It was as if the real Adam, *her Adam*, had been taken away—snatched up by aliens or something equally crazy—so that she was left with this robot-like hulk instead.

Once I get the breathing figured out, it'll just be a matter of finding a way to keep my smile in place until all these people have gone.

If only she had a good excuse to walk out, too. Claire wanted to be whisked away—to vanish into thin air.

Then, as she stood there, fighting for composure, she heard a baby's lusty cry and she'd never felt more relieved. The corners of her mouth lifted into a tiny smile. This was exactly what she needed.

Approaching the nearby group of guests, she said, 'I'm afraid you'll have to excuse me for a little while. I need to give the baby, Rosco, his bottle. But, please, stay and help yourselves to coffee, more drink...cake...'

The smile stayed in place as she hurried towards the nursery.

Adam was tired and drained from another restless night, but he rose, as he always did before six. To fill in time before he could make a phone call, he went for a jog around the outskirts of Daybreak.

An hour later, he was sitting at Jack's kitchen table drinking a mug of tea when Jack lumbered sleepily into the room and shoved a piece of paper under his nose.

'Here's Sally's telephone number.'

Adam's eyes narrowed as he studied the digits. 'That's a Brisbane number.'

'Yes. So what?'

'I've tried stacks of people in Brisbane and no one could tell me where she was.'

Pulling out a chair, Jack flopped into it.

'Sal chose to go underground for some reason. Probably because of the baby, I suppose. This number belongs to a broken-down old journalist, who's pretty much out of circulation these days. I've met him once or twice at Sally's parties. She's been friends with him for ages. Now that he's retired and lives on a part pension, she cooks his meals in exchange for a room and a quiet life.'

'How long's she been living there?'

Jack shrugged before reaching for the heavy china teapot and pouring himself a mug of Adam's strong brew. 'About three months. Since she gave up her job at the paper.'

Frowning, Adam said, 'You know a lot about Sally. A hell of a lot more than either Claire or I have been able to find out for months now.'

'It might look that way, but I only know the edited version of what she's been up to—what she's been prepared to tell me. I certainly didn't know she was pregnant.' Jack took a sip of tea, pulled a grimacing face and then stirred in two spoonfuls of sugar.

As Adam watched he said, 'Listen, mate. It might be better if you ring Sally.'

The spoon in Jack's hand stilled. 'Why?'

'Well, if she feels she's got to hide from Claire and

me for some crazy reason, she's not going to be thrilled to have me hunting her down, is she?'

Jack seemed to consider this for a moment. 'I guess not.' He sighed. 'But you want me to ask her who her baby's father is? That's mighty personal—about as personal as you can get.'

'How do you feel about asking?' It was a question Adam hadn't needed to ask. The answer was already there in the bleakness of Jack's normally cheerful face.

'Not too happy.'

Adam looked at his brother thoughtfully. 'Jack—about you and Sally. I thought perhaps you— You two haven't got a thing going, have you?'

Jack went very still. 'A thing? What kind of thing? You're usually a bit more articulate than that, big brother.'

'You know what I'm talking about. To quote Sally, herself—I'm talking about girl-guy stuff. A relationship.'

Half of Jack's face seemed to slip sideways as if he failed in an attempt to smile. 'No chance for me there, mate. Sally's all for the big smoke. She a complete city chick. I'm not her type at all.'

The two brothers sat in silence. Jack wrapped his big hands around his mug and twisted it back and forth on the table-top.

'I guess you don't feel you know her well enough to broach a rather private question about her baby,' Adam suggested.

Jack looked relieved. 'Yeah, that's right.'

'OK, then. I'll speak to her.'

'If she hears what's happened to you and Claire she'll be devastated.'

'Yes. I guess she will.'

Snatching up the piece of paper, Adam braced his

shoulders and crossed to the phone on the kitchen counter. It was so damn ridiculous that he felt nervous. There had been times when he should have been nervous and he hadn't, such as in his late teens when he'd tried the rodeo circuit for a season or two.

But riding wild bulls, even Terminator, the most bad-tempered of them all, hadn't made him feel as anxious as he did now. His marriage teetered on the brink of collapse and could be saved by this phone call.

There was an answer on the third ring. 'Vince Blainey,' a husky voice wheezed.

'Good morning, Vince.' Adam spoke as brightly as he could, given that his stomach felt as if it were imploding. 'I'm trying to contact Sally Tremaine and I understand she can be reached on this number.'

'What's your name?' the voice snapped.

'Adam Townsend,' he said politely although he felt like snapping back. 'I'm Sally's brother-in-law.'

'Yeah, I know about you.' The surly response didn't sound promising.

'So can you help me?'

'I'm sorry, mate, I can't.'

Adam rolled his eyes to the ceiling and shook his head. He glanced Jack's way as he said, 'I need to speak to Sally about a very important matter. A family matter.'

Old Vince Blainey didn't sound particularly sympathetic. 'Maybe you do, but she's not here.'

'Then can you give me her forwarding address? Somewhere I can contact her.'

''Fraid not.'

'This is a matter of some urgency.'

Jack's chair scraped as he stood and crossed the kitchen to stand beside Adam. 'No luck?' he asked softly.

Covering the phone's mouthpiece, Adam muttered,

'He's giving me a load of bull—but I'm sure he knows where she is.'

Jack sighed. 'Maybe I'd better speak to him after all.'

He took the receiver and Adam watched as he spoke.

'Vince, it's Jack here. Listen, mate, this is pretty serious. We really do need to track down Sally.'

There was a lengthy silence as Jack listened and Adam felt even more anxious as he watched his brother's face grow puzzled and then completely baffled.

CHAPTER THIRTEEN

FORTUNATELY, the road from Nardoo to Daybreak was bitumen for most of the ninety kilometre trip and it was so familiar to Claire she felt she knew every tree and clump of grass along the roadside.

She usually enjoyed the journey, watching out for familiar landmarks—the enormous ghost gum that stood beside the neighbour's mailbox, the stand of ancient paperbarks circling the billabong down on the flat, the glimpses of the river flashing in the sunlight as it curled its way across the plains. But this afternoon she hardly noticed anything except the road ahead.

During her hour-long journey, the sun moved further to the west and the afternoon shadows lengthened, tiger-striping the road and softening the surrounding bush, but Claire paid little attention. This afternoon she was a woman on a mission. A mission that filled her with dread.

It had taken her all day to pluck up the courage to drive to Jack's in search of Adam. The morning had been taken up with the aftermath of the party. She and Nancy had provided a tropical breakfast for overnight guests and, with the help of the nieces, they had completed the general post-party clean-up.

By the early evening, Claire was exhausted but she knew she couldn't sit by herself at Nardoo a minute longer. She needed Adam. She had to find him. Now. And once the decision was made, she didn't waste any time on second thoughts.

She was going to find her husband and, God help her,

she'd work out a way to win him back. Securing Rosco in his baby capsule in the back of the car, she tossed in a bag of baby essentials and headed straight for town.

It wasn't until she reached the turn-off to the main road that she realised Adam might not be at Jack's any more, but she couldn't bring herself to turn back at that point.

Her pride was in tatters and she didn't care how pathetic her behaviour might look to others. She was going to find Adam and beg him to come back. She would apologise profusely, she would forgive him *anything* if only he would come home with her.

She knew that if she'd confided in some of her friends, they would have rolled their eyes at her weakness, but the role of the injured wife just didn't work for Claire any more. She'd tried it for the week before Adam had left and it had been the most soul-destroying week of her life. She was rather ashamed of how badly she'd handled the whole business.

Maybe she still couldn't bear to think of Adam sleeping with Sally, but she knew without a shadow of a doubt that living without him was far, far worse.

The trip into town seemed to take much longer than usual, but eventually the road narrowed to a single lane as it wound its way down into a little gully and at last she was rattling over the bridge that crossed Daybreak Creek.

Her heart began to thump. In fifteen minutes she would reach Jack's place. In fifteen minutes she would have to find the words to persuade Adam that he had to come home.

She knew the task she faced wasn't easy. Last night Adam had been as cold and remote as Antarctica, but now she told herself she could do this.

She could find a way to make him listen. To make him

understand that she was sorry. Sorry? She was flattened with remorse.

Catching sight of her hair in the rear-view mirror, she gave it a hurried comb with her fingers. Perhaps it had been a mistake not to take any special care with her appearance. But last night she'd looked her best and it hadn't helped one jot! So today she hadn't bothered to change out of her faded old work jeans and grey tee shirt. And she hadn't bothered with make-up.

This wasn't a mission to be accomplished via feminine wiles. This was a time for wearing her heart on her sleeve so that Adam couldn't miss her message.

As he approached Daybreak Creek Adam slowed his truck to a halt at the give-way sign. The setting sun glinted fiercely in his eyes but he was sure he'd caught sight of a car coming from the opposite direction and approaching the narrow, single-lane bridge.

He squinted at the sun's blinding force and raised his hand to block out the glare, but he still couldn't be sure if there was a vehicle approaching. Then he heard the rattle of wheels on the bridge and knew he'd been right to wait.

He watched it emerge out of the glare as it reached the end of the bridge and accelerated past him, up the incline away from the creek. *Hang about!* His mouth dropped open as he watched it hurtle past. That was *his* car! It was the dark green late-model sedan he and Claire laughingly called their city car.

He caught a flashing glimpse of Claire in the driver's seat and his heart tripped as he recognised the familiar golden hair and the delicate profile he knew so intimately. Her eyes were fixed dead ahead. She didn't give him so much as a passing glance.

With a flash of alarm, he gripped the steering wheel more tightly and turned to watch the vehicle disappear over the brow of the hill.

This was crazy! How could she have missed seeing him as he'd pulled off to the side of the road to let her pass? She knew his truck so well, she would have recognised it. What was her problem that she was so focused on the narrow road in front of her she didn't look to right or left? And why the heck was she driving to Daybreak at this late hour?

He was on his way back to Nardoo! He'd been planning to tell her he couldn't stay away a minute longer.

To tell her he'd spoken to Sally.

A noisy sigh of exasperation escaped. This part of the road was too narrow and the scrub in this particular stretch was too heavily timbered and close to the road for him to do a U-turn. He couldn't follow her until he found a safe place to turn around.

By then she would be well ahead. She could be at Jack's place by the time he reached her. Damn! There was so much he needed to tell her—but he'd wanted to talk to her in the privacy of their own home.

He had to explain how stupid and wrong he'd been to leave her. No matter how bad things had seemed, he should have stayed at her side. She was *his wife*. Nothing could be gained by separation. Nothing except wretched, aching despair.

He had no idea how she was feeling but he couldn't let himself think about the possibility that she wouldn't take him back.

It took five minutes of driving in the wrong direction before the road widened enough to give him turning space. Dusk was hurrying in now. By the time he reached the creek again, the gully was dark and shadowy, out of the reach of the sinking sun. In the trees along the creek banks, the usual flocks of noisy corellas and cockatoos gathered to squabble and fuss as they did every evening.

Nightfall was almost complete by the time he caught up to Claire's car. He followed her tail lights through the little scattering of five acre hobby farms on the outskirts of Daybreak until they eventually pulled up behind his brother's house, an old, low set Queenslander at one end of Daybreak's main street. There were lights on in nearly every room.

Stepping out of his truck and slamming the door shut, Adam walked towards Claire's car, his riding boots crunching on the gravel.

He was sure she must have known he'd been following her and she had to be able to hear his approach, but she showed no sign. She remained sitting perfectly still, staring out through the windscreen and gripping the top of the steering wheel with both hands.

When he was level with her, he bent down to look through the driver's window. Her perfect profile was silhouetted by the background lights from the house. One look at the tension in her face and Adam's instincts told him it would be best to take this lightly. He tried for a joke. 'Could I see your licence, please, driver?'

Slowly her face turned his way. 'But—but, Constable,' she retaliated with a grim, lifeless attempt at a smile, as if the effort to joke cost her a great deal, 'I wasn't speeding.'

'Perhaps you were driving under the influence.'

After only the slightest hesitation, she asked, 'You want to give me a breath test?'

She sounded so breathless, he doubted she would have any air left to test.

'That's right.'

Claire's door opened and she climbed stiffly out of the car and turned to face him, but she looked scared and she kept the open driver's door between them like a barrier.

This wasn't quite how he'd pictured their reunion. He'd planned on finding Claire at home. In the nursery at Nardoo or the study, perhaps the garden. He'd imagined walking to her across the lawn. She would be kneeling on a little mat, attacking weeds, and when she heard him call her name she would leap to her feet, her face lit with joy. Something that demanded violins playing in the background.

She was always such a romantic and he'd even entertained the ridiculous fantasy that she might see him as the hero returning home to reclaim his wife…the stuff of legends.

Forget legends. Here he was, standing on the edge of the road—an ordinary bloke, who'd stuffed up his marriage, facing an angry wife. He felt anything but heroic.

'So what brings you into Daybreak?' he asked.

'I was coming to see you,' Claire said. Despite the encroaching darkness, he could see the way her dark eyes shone with tears. Her hands clutched the top of the door so tightly her white knuckles looked about to snap with the effort. 'Why were you on the road?'

'I was going back to Nardoo to see you,' Adam said, trying to put a wealth of reassurance into his voice.

'Oh.'

He swallowed, but there was something in his throat that wouldn't go away. 'I've seen Sally—'

Her head swung to stare at the house. 'Sally's here at Jack's?'

'Yeah. She arrived this afternoon—a couple of hours ago.'

'I see,' was all she said, but her right hand flew to cover her heart, as if she was trying to still its wild beating. 'So—so you've spoken to her?'

'Of course.'

She closed her eyes and Adam was certain she was garnering strength for her next question. It came in a whisper. 'What did she say?'

'Sally's willing to swear on a stack of Bibles that I'm not the father of her child.'

At first he thought she hadn't heard him. There was no answering smile, no sign of her relief. But her cheeks grew very pink and her eyes opened wide as she asked, 'Did she tell you who Rosco's father is?'

Adam's fists clenched. 'No.'

The colour left her cheeks as her face blanched. 'Why won't she tell you? *Why?*' A desperate sigh escaped her. 'Why on earth won't she clear this up?'

'Because when I left her an hour ago, she still hadn't told the father in question. She felt she should tell him first.'

'Oh?' she said again, her voice rising with curiosity. 'So when will she do that? Why did she have to waste time coming back to Daybreak?'

He shrugged. He had a very good idea he knew exactly why Sally was here, but, respecting her wishes, he kept his thoughts to himself. 'I've taken a stab in the dark and deduced that the father must live here.'

'Surely not.' Her eyes scanned the quiet street before she turned and looked into the back of the car. For the first time, Adam noticed the baby capsule and little Rosco curled up asleep. With his soft dark hair, chubby cheeks and tiny starfish hands, he was a miniature portrait of innocence.

Her pale lips trembled. 'What did you talk about with Sally? Do you know if she wants Rosco back?'

He didn't answer immediately, but there was no avoiding her question. 'I'd say there's a chance.'

'A good chance?'

Adam reached out and touched her hand as it gripped the door. She didn't snatch it away and so, gently, he traced each whitened knuckle with the pads of his fingers. 'We're not the only ones who've been having a rough time of it lately. I'd say becoming a mother was a much more powerful experience than Sally anticipated.'

To his surprise, Claire gripped his hand with both of hers. 'I'm sure you're right,' she whispered. 'I've been thinking about it a lot. I've been thinking about Sally and I'm sure she has to be absolutely miserable without her baby. He's such a dear little fellow and he's *hers*.'

Sudden tears shone in her eyes. 'God, Adam, can you imagine how awful that would be? To give birth to a gorgeous little baby like Rosco and then to give him away?'

Adam groaned in sympathy. If only he could make her world right. If only it were simply a matter of kissing away her tears. 'Could you bear to give him back?' he asked.

Before she answered, the front door of Jack's house opened and light streamed down the front path.

'Adam, is that you out there?' Jack called.

'Yes,' he replied. 'Claire's here, too.'

'Then, for Pete's sake, come on in.'

'We're coming.'

As he released Claire he said, 'I'll help you with the baby.'

But she placed a restraining hand on his arm as he reached for the back door handle.

'He's still sound asleep and he'll be perfectly safe in the car for a minute or two. Perhaps we should go in and let Sally fetch him. That way she can have a moment alone with her little boy. It might be easier for her, without us.'

Adam smiled and he couldn't resist dropping a swift kiss on her nose. 'That's a very thoughtful suggestion. Just demonstrates yet again that there's more to my—to you than a great body and a beautiful face.'

He was rewarded by a shaky smile. 'Maybe I'm just a coward,' Claire admitted. 'It will save me from having to hand him over.' She reached for Adam's hand. 'This could be the end of my experience of motherhood.'

He squeezed her cold fingers, wishing there were words of comfort he could offer, but unable to find them.

Together they walked up the weedy path to find a rather pale-faced Jack waiting on the top step.

'I wondered if you two might show up,' he said, looking so strained it was hard to tell whether or not he was pleased to see them.

Behind him in the lounge, Sally was sitting on the sofa. Her face was red and blotchy from crying. She looked utterly miserable. At the first sight of her sister, Claire burst past Jack and hurried across the room.

And just as spontaneously Sally shot out of her seat to meet her. The sisters collided in the middle of the room and clung together like war orphans reunited after years in prison camps. It was the extravagant kind of coming together that Adam had envisaged earlier for himself and Claire.

He watched the two women hugging and crying and then turned slightly to catch his brother's eye. But Jack was staring at the women and looking a little worse for wear, as if he had a hangover—or was suffering from shock. Adam suspected the latter was more likely.

He stepped closer and slapped a brotherly hand on Jack's shoulder. 'Is everything OK, mate?'

Jack's dazed blue eyes met his. 'I guess I'm sort of OK,' he muttered. 'And I'm sort of—' he paused as if searching for words, but it seemed that tonight words were beyond him '—sort of *not* OK.'

'When did you get home?'

'About half an hour ago. I've been tied up at Glebe Downs for most of the day testing for tuberculosis.'

Adam gave his brother another sympathetic pat. He was certain that in the past half-hour Jack had come face to face with one or two shocks. No wonder his face looked as pale as a poached egg.

Claire and Sally released each other and Sally looked across at the men and rubbed at her streaming eyes. 'What a tear-jerker of an afternoon!' she sobbed. 'I've already cried all over poor Adam and then Jack and now I've saturated Claire. I'm sure I must be dehydrated by now.'

'Well, there's one more person for you to cry over,' Claire said gently.

Sally gasped and her eyes grew so round they looked as if they might pop. 'Have you brought *him*?'

'Rosco? Of course we did. He's outside in the car. I thought you might like to fetch him in.'

'Oh, yes!' Sally whispered breathlessly and her face grew white, making the red, swollen blotches stand out even more brightly. 'Oh, my goodness. Oh, crumbs, I've missed my little man so much. I'm shaking!'

'Go on out to him,' Claire urged as she handed her the car keys.

'But...' Sally frowned. 'Does this mean...?'

For a brief second, Claire pressed her lips together before she smiled bravely. 'It means I'm bringing him back to you, Sal.'

'Oh, Claire.' Sally began to cry again as she gave her sister another fierce hug. Claire pushed her away gently and Sally took three steps across the room towards the door, but then she turned to Jack and held out a shaking hand to him. 'You come, too,' she said and her eyes glowed warmly.

Jack hesitated. For the count of five, he stood staring at Sally, scratching at his shirt front in a distracted way.

Claire shot Adam a startled glance.

Finally, Jack blinked and said, 'Sure, I'll come.' And, together, he and Sally hurried outside.

Adam watched Claire and she turned to him, her beautiful dark eyes wide and sparkling with tears and curiosity. She stepped towards him.

Neither spoke. Standing close together but conscious of not touching, they watched Jack and Sally reach the end of the path.

The light from the house didn't quite reach the footpath and there was no street light nearby, so for a moment the other couple were swallowed by darkness. Then the car's interior light came on as Jack opened the door.

They saw the silhouette of Sally's and Jack's bodies standing close together, looking into the car. Then Sally's head drooped onto Jack's shoulder and she was trembling and Jack's arms came around her and they were clinging to each other.

'Oh, Adam,' Claire sobbed and she rubbed her wet face against his sleeve.

Gently, Adam steered her towards the kitchen. 'I don't think we should be watching what happens out there.'

They paused in the kitchen doorway and Claire looked

up at him, her eyes filled to overflowing with emotion. 'Are you thinking what I'm thinking?'

'About my little brother and your little sister?'

'And a little baby.'

'Who looks exactly like Jack.'

Claire shook her head as she smiled ruefully. 'You and Jack are so alike. Why didn't we think of that ages ago?'

'Well, I have to say it did occur to me as the most likely answer, but poor Jack's been kept in the dark, so I was a bit hamstrung.'

Claire shook her head. 'I hope Sally hasn't hurt him.'

'If she has, I think she wants to make amends. Big time.'

'I'm going to put on some coffee,' Claire said quickly. 'I think good strong coffee might be needed all round.'

'With perhaps a hefty slug of brandy for Jack,' Adam suggested with a crooked grin.

Numb with surprise at the turn of events, Claire surveyed Jack's kitchen. Unwashed dishes littered the sink. A solitary, blackened banana rested in the dusty fruit bowl and the table-top was hard to find beneath a jumble of newspapers and veterinary journals. When he dined at home, Jack clearly liked to read as he ate.

From experience, she knew that delving into the contents of his fridge and pantry could be a risky business, but one item he could always be relied on to have in stock was good quality coffee. Now as she filled the coffee-maker she said to Adam, 'I wonder how Sally and Jack really feel about each other.'

'They are probably right in the middle of sorting that out now.'

'Poor things,' she said as she hunted for four clean mugs, gave up and began to rinse some under the hot-water tap.

Adam leaned a broad shoulder against the doorjamb and one eyebrow rose. 'Hopefully, they won't be poor things at all,' he said. 'With luck, they'll discover they're madly in love.' He smiled enigmatically. 'And if that's the case, they could take some time.'

Claire couldn't help frowning as she reached for a tea towel. 'The problem is Sally's such a city slicker.'

'And Jack's such a hayseed.'

'Yes.'

'I guess that's always been a problem for them. Solving it won't be easy.' He frowned. 'Speaking of problems,' he said cautiously, 'we've got problems of our own to sort out.'

And suddenly Claire felt as if they had slammed into a brick wall—an impossible wall of pent-up emotion. She placed the mugs carefully on the bench. There was nothing else to be said about Sally and Jack.

What were they doing gossiping about their sister and brother when they had their own relationship to deal with? Not one word of reconciliation had been exchanged.

She was suddenly nervous. She and Adam were together and alone and yet, when they stopped talking about Sally and Jack, she felt they were still oceans apart.

When she'd left Nardoo, she'd thought everything would fall into place like in a romantic movie. They would take one look at each other and fall into each other's arms. She would beg his forgiveness and he would give it gladly.

But right now he wasn't looking very approachable. He hadn't yet entered the kitchen, but remained glued against the door frame. His throat worked and his eyes pierced hers as he said, 'You said you were driving into Daybreak to see me.'

Nodding, she twisted her hands in front of her. She stood beside the big, old pine table that dominated the kitchen while she struggled to remember her prepared speech. Gripping the back of a chair as tightly as she'd gripped the car door earlier, she said, 'I came because I had something very important to tell you.'

One corner of Adam's mouth tilted crookedly. 'I'm here and I'm all ears.'

This was it. Time to deliver the speech. But it seemed so long ago that she'd left Nardoo, when her mind had been clear and focused. Everything felt different now.

Her mouth trembled into a tiny, embarrassed smile. 'I drove all the way into Daybreak to tell you—to ask you to forgive me, Adam. I'm so sorry I didn't trust you. I can't believe I made you go away.'

Her heart stood still as she waited for his response. He didn't rush to scoop her into his arms. He merely accepted her words with a slight nod.

'I take some blame too,' he said. 'I shouldn't have gone. I should never have walked out on our marriage. Not even for a day.'

'I was so stupid, Adam. I—I don't blame you for walking out. I don't blame you for being mad at me. I should have trusted you.'

His eyes regarded her gently. 'It's pretty hard for a marriage to survive without trust.'

Claire covered her face with her hands. Now that she knew the simple truth about Jack, she felt so ashamed of the way she'd carried on. But at the time, her fears had seemed justified.

Lifting her head, she tried to explain. 'The problem was I knew that you would do anything to make me happy and so, when I saw Rosco, I became afraid of what that *anything* might mean. I was frightened I'd asked for too much—that I'd pushed you into…'

'Getting together with Sally?'

'I shouldn't have freaked out. You told me you hadn't—*done anything* with Sally—and I should have believed you. But I want you to know that even before I got here and saw Jack and Sally together, I was coming to tell you that it didn't matter any more who Rosco's father is, because—'

She paused and blinked away tears.

'Because?' His voice vibrated with tension.

Claire sniffed and pushed a tendril of hair away from her eye. 'Because I've realised that you're more important to me than any baby. It wouldn't matter what you had done. I need you. I love you.'

She heard his choking cry as he took a step into the room.

'Oh, Adam!'

They stood transfixed, staring at each other, their eyes searching hungrily for a sign. Claire couldn't bear it. She held her arms out to Adam, imploring him to come to her.

And now at last he lunged forward and pulled her savagely against him. She sank against his lovely strength as he pressed his lips to her forehead. 'Claire, darling. Oh, sweetheart, I've missed you.'

They clung together, laughing and crying simultaneously. Adam's mouth sought hers and his kiss was hungry, deep, happy. Bruising her, loving her. It was what she'd longed for. Their urgent, lonely bodies pressed close and closer, heart to heart. Healing in the warmth of each other's love.

It was so good to be standing in the middle of Jack's messy kitchen, becoming happy again.

Happy? Claire was ecstatic. This was Adam. Her Adam.

Could her feet possibly be touching the ground? They weren't! Adam had lifted her high against him. Quickly, she wound her legs around his and covered his face and neck with a shower of happy kisses. She kissed the underside of his jaw, his ear lobe, his cheek, his sexy, full lower lip, then his top lip, both lips, the cleft in his chin. Another kiss for his chin.

And Adam was kissing her too as he held her effortlessly in his strong arms and somehow they melted together onto a kitchen chair with Claire still locked against him, straddling his lap.

With a small cry of triumph, she drew his head towards her and kissed him deeply, taking charge, holding both sides of his face and tasting him, tasting how clean and warm and so especially hers he was, glorying in the hard, masculine feel of his body, pressing him against the back of the chair, wanting him now in Jack's kitchen even though Sally and Jack might walk in at any minute.

And then she couldn't help herself. She had to push into him, feeling his body respond, hearing his ragged breathing match hers, shivering deliciously as his hands reached for her and made private explorations that seemed strangely daring and exciting, as awe-inspiring as their very first time together.

On the explosive edge of losing her head completely, she heard footsteps in the room next door.

'Oh, dear,' she muttered. She was shaking a little as her head sank against Adam's shoulder. Then she grinned and dropped another kiss on his mouth before pulling her tee shirt into place and wriggling off his lap.

'Now what was I doing?' she mumbled. On the bench

behind her, the coffee-maker gurgled and popped. She smiled. 'Oh, yeah. Now I remember.'

With a small, confidential grin, Adam propped a nonchalant elbow on the table and made a pretence of reading an out-of-date catalogue for a bull sale. Claire tried to look busy as she rattled around in the cutlery drawer searching for teaspoons.

'Mmm, that coffee smells good,' came Jack's voice from just beyond the doorway.

Claire turned to find him coming into the room smiling broadly. She wanted to rush to him and hug him. Was he as happy as she was? Uncertainty held her back. What had happened out at the car?

She was suddenly afraid for her sister and she felt the kind of nervous excitement she hadn't felt since her school days—waiting for exam results.

'So what do you think of the baby?' she asked.

Jack's grin widened. 'He's terrific.'

'And Sal's OK?'

'I'm terrific, too,' Sally said, stepping beside Jack into the kitchen. Rosco was in her arms and her face was alight with joy.

'Do you think Rosco looks well?' Claire asked. 'I've looked after him as carefully as I could.'

'He looks wonderful,' Sally reassured her. 'Better than I remembered. I'm sure he's grown. Thank you so much for everything you've done.'

Claire looked fondly at the little baby boy cuddled against her sister's breast, so soft and warm...so wriggly and alert...so tiny and perfect...so helpless and yet so full of potential...

Her eyes lingered on him, admiring again his tiny, perfect features—sleepy dark eyes, baby-fine dark hair and sweet rosy lips. If she had a baby, he would probably look just like that…

For a moment the old pain returned. The emptiness, the longing… There was a good chance she would never be really free of that sense of loss.

'Here, take a seat,' she said quickly. 'I'll pour the coffee.'

'Thanks.'

While the others took seats around the old pine table, she set out the mugs, the coffee-pot, a sugar bowl and spoons. Jack's kitchenware didn't run to milk jugs so she had to put the cardboard carton beside them, then she took her own seat, opposite Adam.

'Well,' she said and looked around at the circle of smiling faces. Smiling, *silent* faces. 'Well, I guess I'll pour the coffee.'

There was a sustained stretch of silence, broken only by little baby snuffles from Rosco and the bubbling sound of pouring coffee. While Jack stashed the newspapers into an erratic pile on the floor, Claire pushed the mugs across the scratched surface of the table. They helped themselves to milk or sugar.

She raised an eyebrow in Adam's direction, but he seemed to be concentrating on his coffee. Sally was gazing at Rosco, her face a picture of serenity and joy like a medieval Madonna's and Jack's face glowed as he watched Sally.

Claire thought she would burst.

'If somebody doesn't say something, I might get violent,' she said loudly.

And so, of course, everybody spoke at once.

'Nice coffee,' Adam said.

'Just what I needed,' added Sally.

'I wonder if I've got anything worth eating,' mused

Jack. 'I think there's some bread and cheese, so I guess we could have toasted sandwiches.'

Dropping her shaking head into her hands, Claire groaned.

Then she heard Sally's husky voice say, 'Chill out, Claire, we're teasing. I take it you'd like me to fill you in on one or two things. Like the latest episode in the silly Sally Tremaine soap opera.'

'I would appreciate that very much.'

She felt Sally's hand squeeze her arm. 'I'm sorry, sis. I know I've put you through a rough time. Where would you like me to start?'

'How about you try the beginning?'

'The beginning as in—?'

'As in how long you and Jack have been an item,' cut in Adam. 'We're presuming Jack is Rosco's old man.'

Sally shot a sultry glance in Jack's direction and grinned. 'We've been seeing each other for quite a while.' After a pause, she added, 'For nearly nine years.'

Claire gasped. 'Nine years? You mean ever since our wedding?'

'On and off.'

'More off than on,' growled Jack.

'Yeah, well. My commitment phobia and our lifestyle differences have caused a few hiccups,' Sally admitted. She reached across the table to slip her small hand inside Jack's beefy fist. 'But the shrew has been well and truly tamed.'

Claire clasped her hands together. 'Does this mean?'

'It means Sally's going to bite the bullet and live with me out here in the sticks.' Jack beamed. '*And* she's going to marry me at long last.'

Sally's grin was as big as a slice of watermelon. 'I've developed a bit of a yen to be a rural reporter.'

There was such a flurry of excited cries and hugs and back-slapping that little Rosco stirred and cried. So then there was a session of baby talk and soothing sounds while his formula was mixed and heated. Jack made a plateful of toasted cheese sandwiches and everyone suddenly realised how hungry they were and dived on them.

Once they were munching happily and Sally was settled and feeding Rosco, she looked very purposefully at Claire and then at Adam.

'Jack's been worried that I've done your marriage permanent damage, but I don't think I need to ask how things are with you guys.' Her face puckered into a smirk. 'You were so busy kissing before that we had to walk back outside and come back stomping our feet before you heard us.'

Claire felt herself blushing as she and Adam exchanged self-conscious grins.

'So I'd better explain about the baby,' Sally said softly.

Claire put her half-eaten sandwich down and her stomach jumped nervously again. 'He's absolutely gorgeous,' she assured her sister, rather unnecessarily.

Sally nodded. 'He certainly is. But, honestly, I really did plan him as a gift for you two. I thought if you can't have a baby of your own, one from Jack and me would be the next best thing—genetically speaking, of course.'

Claire didn't think it was the time or the place to explain to her sister how much heartache that genetic connection had caused.

'But,' continued Sally, 'I mucked it up by not telling Jack what I was doing.'

'So you didn't know last summer that you were making a donation to us?' Adam teased his brother.

'Hell, no,' Jack exclaimed. His eyes softened as he looked again at Sally holding Rosco.

'And the thing I didn't know,' added Sally, 'is the massive impact this little being would have on me. Carrying him for all that time—and the birth!' She bit her lip, looking suddenly uncomfortable, the way women always did when it came to discussing pregnancies or birth in front of Claire. 'It was a very grown-up, life-changing kind of experience,' she finished and she'd never looked more serious.

No one spoke for a moment or two. It was as if they were all taking in the fact that Sally Tremaine's wild days were quite clearly behind her.

Claire realised that the past ten months had been an enlightening journey for her sister as well as for her.

'But how do you two feel?' Sally asked. 'About handing Rosco back, I mean.'

Claire's and Adam's gazes met and they smiled at each other. From blue eyes to brown flowed a sense of renewed connection and Claire could feel once again the powerful force of their strong love and close understanding.

Maybe she would never have a baby and perhaps her heart would always be faintly shadowed by a sense of loss, but she knew that at long last she could live with this loss and even, in time, rise above it.

She felt perfectly calm as she turned back to Sally and said, 'Apart from the fact that you *must* have him, we're sure that we *want* you to have him. Rosco belongs with his parents.'

'Thank you so much,' whispered Sally and fresh tears began to fall. 'I think your gift of—of giving my baby back—' she sobbed '—is so much harder than any effort I made.'

Slipping off her chair, Claire knelt beside her sister

and hugged her. 'No, darling,' she said. 'It's not hard for me when I know this is exactly where he belongs.'

'And just remember we want first call when you need babysitters,' Adam chipped in. 'Claire and I make a great aunt and uncle combination.'

CHAPTER FOURTEEN

ADAM left his truck at Jack's place and drove home to Nardoo in Claire's sedan. She curled happily on the passenger's seat and occasional patches of moonlight allowed him to catch little glimpses of her face. She looked wistful and dreamy. Was she thinking about the baby she'd had for such a short time and then lost?

With any luck she wouldn't be thinking about that at all, she'd be thinking about making love. After that heated exchange in Jack's kitchen, he'd been hard pressed to think of anything else.

He took his eyes off the road to glance at her again. 'A penny for your thoughts.'

She didn't answer at first but then she smiled archly as she said, ' I've been wondering what you thought of the outfit I wore for your party.'

Adam laughed. That would teach him to be vain. He'd been waiting for Claire to tell him again how much she fancied him. Instead she wanted to hear how much he fancied her. Not that it mattered. He was more than happy to oblige.

'You looked sensational, but it should be declared illegal for women to dress like that in public.'

'Illegal? Why?'

'Every fellow there was fantasising about you. There's something about the dress that makes it look transparent. I kept imagining I could see through it.'

'Could you?'

'Unfortunately, no.'

179

Turning her way, he saw Claire's pleased, almost smug smile.

'But that didn't stop me from seeing it coming off,' he added.

That made her sit up. 'You mean you could picture yourself undressing me?'

'Better than that. I could see myself watching you while *you* took it off.'

She leaned closer to him and as she draped her arm along the back of his seat her breathless little laugh sent waves of hot blood pounding through his body.

'Tell me about it,' she asked huskily. 'How did I undress?'

He couldn't help smiling. He should have guessed that Claire would jump at the chance to play a teasing sexy game despite the fact that they were driving in the dark along a lonely outback road.

'That outfit was actually a separate skirt and top, wasn't it?' he asked.

'Good heavens, Adam. Did you notice little details like that?'

'I sure did.'

'But you hardly looked at me all night.'

'Don't you believe it.'

She sat in silence for twenty seconds or so, obviously thinking about his comments, and her mouth curved in an enigmatic smile as she stared dreamily at the road ahead. Then her voice turned silky as she murmured, 'So what did you see? What did I take off first?'

His hands locked around the steering wheel. 'Claire, you'll cause an accident.'

'Come on,' she urged. 'Don't be a spoilsport. Tell me.'

He took a deep breath. 'The skirt.'

'Did I lower the zip very, very slowly and then step out of it?'

Adam gulped. 'Yeah. And then you just stood there looking incredibly sexy in high-heeled shoes with no stockings—just your long, slinky legs all bare.'

'And gold silk panties.'

Adam groaned. 'If you don't stop, woman, I'm going to pull over and start undressing you on the edge of the road.'

'Actually,' Claire murmured, 'those panties were more see-through lace than silk.'

'Claire!'

'And I wasn't wearing a bra.'

'Stop tormenting me.'

'I'm sorry.'

She didn't sound sorry in the slightest, but as he swung the car off the main road and onto the track leading into Nardoo she lapsed into silence again.

'Nearly home,' he said, thinking of bed...and Claire in there with him...and wanting her to know how very, very happy he felt tonight.

'You know,' he said, with his eyes on the bumpy track ahead, 'I'm still madly in love with you, Claire. It's not a settled, comfortably married feeling at all. I—' How could he explain the vital and urgent need he felt for her? 'It's like I'm burning—do you understand?'

She didn't answer.

'Claire?'

Turning to look at her, he discovered she had fallen asleep. Even as he watched her head lolled sideways until it came to rest on his shoulder.

'Sleeping Beauty,' he whispered with a wry grin as he negotiated the vehicle through the black night. Actually, when he thought about the way she'd been teasing him, Sleeping Wicked Fairy was more appropriate.

But he was content for now to enjoy the gentle pressure of her head on his shoulder and the silky feel of her soft curls brushing his neck.

She was still asleep when they pulled to a halt at the foot of the homestead's front steps.

'Claire,' he said softly, giving her a gentle nudge. 'We're home.'

She didn't move.

Smiling ruefully, Adam looked at her. Her dark lashes didn't flicker as they lay in thick half-moons against her pale cheeks. Her breathing was deep and slow. He gave her one more little shake. 'Time for bed, Claire.'

Again there was no sign that she heard him. He told himself that it was hardly surprising that she was exhausted. She hadn't had a decent night's sleep since Rosco had arrived and then there'd been all the work for the party, plus the emotional ordeal of handing the baby back to Sally.

She probably needed to sleep for a week.

Lifting her out of the car, he carried her up the steps, pushed the unlocked front door open with his shoulder and carried her down the hallway to their bedroom. When he laid her gently on the bed, she still didn't stir.

A chuckle bubbled low in his throat. He'd left Jack's place earlier this afternoon, full of plans to come home to an emotional reunion and a night of passionate making-up.

Now, when he brushed his lips across Claire's relaxed mouth, there wasn't a glimmer of a response. She lay like a rag doll, dead to the world.

Not a chance of passion.

He pulled off her shoes and socks. 'You're a wicked

little temptress,' he whispered and he lowered the zipper on her jeans, gently dragged them down till she lay in nothing but her tee shirt and panties. 'But I love you.'

He longed to touch her. Wanted her so badly! Remembering again the conversation in the car, he groaned. It was hard to see the funny side of this—the ironic contrast between Claire's teasing fantasy and this frustrating reality.

However, there was nothing to do but to draw the sheet up to her chin, undress and take a cold shower and prepare for a night of torture. After a week of painful separation, he had to lie next to his exquisitely sexy wife while he let her sleep the deep sleep she justly deserved.

Claire woke, out of habit, at first light and lay for a few puzzled minutes, trying to remember what had happened the night before. The last thing she remembered was driving home from Jack's place. They'd waved happy farewells to Sally and Jack as the couple had stood at Jack's front door with blissful arms wrapped around each other.

But she couldn't remember anything about arriving back at Nardoo. How had she got into bed? Why was she still in her tee shirt?

She rolled sideways…and smiled softly as she discovered the man in her bed. A dark-haired, sleeping man, as beautiful as a Greek god.

Wow! This was her favourite fantasy. She nestled into her pillow as she lay on her side and gazed at him. He really was something. She'd always fancied guys with those cute dimples in their chins. Should she dare to lift the sheet and take a peek at the rest of him?

Of course she should.

Kneeling, she pulled away the fine white sheet and gasped as she uncovered the startling beauty of this naked man. From his broad shoulders and deeply muscled chest, feathered with dark hair, to his slim waist, narrow hips and strong, long legs, he was every inch a god.

Every inch!

What would he do if he woke up and found her naked beside him? The very thought made her limp with longing. But it was an irresistible thought. Still in her kneeling position, she slowly pulled her tee shirt over her head.

And as she tossed it aside the god's eyes opened. She was staring into deep blue eyes. She was diving into them…drowning in them… He was bone-melting gorgeous!

She wanted to touch him. Needed him to touch her.

'Good morning,' he said, smiling.

'Good morning.'

He reached towards her and sent delicious shivers over her skin as he traced the line of her collar-bone. 'Do you always look this good in the mornings?'

She felt her cheeks and several other parts of her body burst into flame. 'I look even better at night.'

His hand massaged her shoulder, slowly, slowly. 'That's impossible.'

Breathless now, she only just managed to reply, 'Hang around, Adonis, and you can find out.'

'The name's Adam,' he said as his other hand reached for her opposite shoulder and he drew her down on top of his long, hard body. 'And I'll hang around just as long as you like. I can promise you that.' Then his hand slid up to her nape and he pulled her head down to his.

'Any other promises?' she whispered as their lips brushed.

With a soft growl, he drew her even closer till his mouth was at her ear and he whispered a drawn-out list of sensational, dazzling promises.

'Oh, Adam,' she whispered huskily.

And he proceeded to carry out each promise.

One by one.

They took rather a long time. The sun had risen well and truly and was streaming in through the deep bay window and spilling across the floor to their bed by the time the final promise was fulfilled and Claire and Adam lay quiet and happy, in no hurry to get on with the working day.

Resting on one elbow, Adam propped his head on his hand as he smiled at Claire and said, 'I still haven't given up, you know.'

She lifted her head to look into his eyes. 'Given up? What do you mean?'

'I mean I still haven't given up hoping we'll have a baby of our own one day.'

'Really? That's a surprise.' It was ridiculous the way her heart leapt.

'I know. It surprises me too, but I feel more confident than ever that we'll have our own baby.'

She sank back against the pillow. 'Wow!' She couldn't help grinning. 'Boy or girl?'

He smiled back at her. 'It's only a feeling, Claire. I'm afraid feelings don't run to details.' Reaching out, he traced the surface of her tummy.

'Adam,' she said quickly, feeling suddenly anxious. She closed her hand over his, stopping its movements. 'You know we can't afford to be carried away by vague feelings. I've had more than my fair share of them in the past.'

But even though she spoke cautiously, she couldn't suppress a little leap of excitement in her chest. Adam was so in tune with the land, with nature. Look at the

way he always knew when it would rain... What if he
was right about this, too?

She released his hand again and watched his face
soften as he rested his brown palm with fingers spread
wide on her pale, flat stomach. It was as if he were feeling something beyond words.

'Maybe I am being foolish,' he said. 'Or maybe our
baby is being conceived right at this minute.'

Claire's breath caught. She couldn't help wondering...hoping...

But no. She knew the pitfalls of that particular track.
'What will be will be,' she said.

Dropping a warm kiss on her forehead, he lifted his
hand from her stomach. Gently he stroked her cheek.
'You're so right.'

'For the time being,' Claire told him, 'I'm just going
to concentrate on you. I'm planning on growing old with
you and I want us to still be a hot item when we join the
grey set, whether we have offspring or not.'

'That sounds so good,' Adam murmured as he dipped
his head and pressed his mouth to the inside of her elbow.
'While you're concentrating on me, would you like me
to give you some hints?'

'Sure.'

'It'll take a while.'

'You have a list?' she asked with a delicious shiver as
he kissed and nibbled his way up her arm.

'Oh, yes, a very, very long list.'

Claire smiled. 'That's fine.' She snuggled closer. 'I
have plenty of time and an excellent memory.'